I focused my peepers on the man leaning against my office door . . .

He filled the room, but he couldn't have weighed more than 165. He removed a cigarette from a black case and deftly lit it. The smoke curled over his tongue like a silk bathrobe. He had a tattoo—a dagger dipped in purple blood—on his left hand. I wondered if he had any more, and where they might be. He said, "Wanda Mallory, P.I., owner of Do It Right Detectives. Home address, 115A Flatbush Avenue, Brooklyn. 130, 5'7". Twenty-eight, red hair, green eyes. Marital status," he smiled, "single."

"More like 127," I said, "first thing in the morning. And you are?" I asked.

"The guy who's going to make you very happy."

"I've heard that before."

"But not from someone who means it."

"Keep going," I said. "I like the way your mouth moves."

He said, "Have you ever heard of Blood & Iron?"

"Motorcycle gang from the East Village."

"And have you ever heard of Strom Bismark?"

I said, "Yeah, I've heard of Strom Bismark. The scurvy dog—smitten so much with his own recidivistic nature that he probably can't piss in the toilet because it's the normal thing to do."

"Recidivistic? What's that?"

"You know, a habitual deviant, criminal. An example of societal ill."

He said, "It's a pleasure to meet you, too."

Books by Valerie Frankel

A Deadline For Murder
Murder On Wheels

Published by POCKET BOOKS

MURDER ON WHEELS

A WANDA MALLORY MYSTERY

VALERIE FRANKEL

POCKET BOOKS

New York   London   Toronto   Sydney   Tokyo   Singapore

An *Original* Publication of POCKET BOOKS

POCKET BOOKS, a division of Simon & Schuster Inc.
1230 Avenue of the Americas, New York, NY 10020

Copyright © 1992 by Valerie Frankel

ISBN: 0-671-73195-5

First Pocket Books printing March 1992

10 9 8 7 6 5 4 3 2 1

POCKET and colophon are registered trademarks of Simon & Schuster Inc.

Cover art and design by Tom McKeveny

Printed in the U.S.A.

Dedicated to
whomever I'm dating right now
(honey, you know it's you)

Special thanks go out to: the family and its newest members, Anna and Sophie; Loretta Fidel, Dana Isaacson, and Leslie Wells for all the yummy lunches; Liz Logan and Carol Schatz for tolerating my other job; Frank Rosenberg for being there; Ellen Tien, Joel Tractenberg, Manny Howard, Nancy Jo Iacoi, and Judy McGuire for many magical moments and stolen lines; and lastly, Glenn Rosenberg, who, in the McDonald's Happy Meal of life, is the prize.

MURDER ON WHEELS

CHAPTER ONE

Shamus Blues

It was a gray Tuesday in January, too cold to take a walk and too early to take a drink. I sat behind my desk at the Do It Right Detective Agency, flipping matchbooks into a hat. I never wear the hat. I'm not a hat person.

The last toss bounced off the brim. If I'd bet against myself, I'd have wheeled out barrels. The steno on my desk listed my New Year's resolutions in red ink. Among them: attempt to quit smoking (unlikely), stop having indiscriminate sex (unfortunately, likely), shop frugally (little choice), and act friendly (out of the question). I hoped it wouldn't take long to break them. Especially the sex one.

I hadn't had a case (or gotten laid) in months. The last one (case) was a routine fidelity check. It ended badly for my client and for me. She lost her husband, and I lost my boyfriend. I cared more than usual, but that's another story. The office hasn't been cleaned in about that long. My circular file overflowed with sticky General Tso's chicken containers, cigarette butts, and empty bottles. Month-old copies of the *Daily Mirror* were piled in one corner by the coat rack.

The subdued-as-orange-can-be carpet needed a vacuum about as much as the whole joint begged for a Handi Wipe. If I had the energy or the inclination, I still wouldn't do it. Straightening had been Alex's job.

I looked out my office window onto Times Square. Smoke rose from the neon Marriott Hotel sign on 45th Street. Exhaust from hundreds of cars turned white from the cold. The air otherwise was thick and black and oppressive as cancer. It's still New York out there, I thought. Heartbreak capital of the world.

There was a knock at the office door—an unexpected jolt out of my quiet, contemplative depression. For a second, I thought it might be Alex, returning to me, begging for my forgiveness. Then, almost instantly, I snapped back to reality. Most likely it was my Brooklyn neighbor and surrogate mother, Santina Epstein. She's a beautician and thinks all my problems will be solved as soon as I get my color chart done. I'd been ducking her for weeks and was still in no mood. The banging didn't stop. I got up slowly and opened the door.

The man gave me the once-over twice. I returned the favor. He was huge—two-eighty, six-five at least, with a wardrobe even more impressive than his girth. He'd covered himself completely in black leather from his motorcycle boots on up—the pants special ordered from Omar the tentmaker. His dark hair was damp and sloppy like squid ink pasta in a colander, and his head was way too small for his bulk. His eyes were just tiny, wet slits on his face. When he pulled off his gloves, I noticed the black half-moons under his fingernails—the sign of a mechanic or a hygienic failure. The only neat thing about him was the beard—it was clipped and combed and a shade lighter than his hair. He smelled of grease, the street, and tanned hide.

"You'll do," he said gruffly, and he reached into the pocket of his pants. He yanked out a wad the size of a lunch box. He peeled off ten bills and handed them to me.

As I counted, I said, "Do you think I'm worth it?" It was $1,000.

"The boss wants to talk to you. Let's go. My bike's downstairs." Surely there wouldn't be room on it for me, unless I was to ride sidesaddle on the handlebars —not my style. I folded the money and pressed it into his palm. I walked back over to my desk and took a seat. My chair is a little too short. My desk is one leg wobbly.

"I listen for free," I said, gesturing at him to sit across from me in the cushy Ethan Allen armchair I keep for clients. He barely fit in it. I didn't apologize for the mess. He didn't start talking. "It's my birthday today," I said. "Have a cigarette with me."

It really was my birthday. I got a nice card and a not-so-nice check from my parents in Florida. Otherwise, jack. The day was still young and it looked like things were beginning to turn. At least I wasn't alone anymore. I spilled a few cigarettes on my desk and we each took one. The barrel flame from my gun lighter (a miniature .38 chiefs Special) shot up too high and threatened to singe his brows. He tilted his head to one side, stoked, and eyed me through the smoke. His first drag nearly exhausted the butt. I smiled and fired my own. I wasn't afraid of him, even if he did outweigh the neighborhood.

I blew smoke at the ceiling and said, "I'm twenty-eight today, and the most important man in my life is Jose Cuervo. I've been feeling more than a little self-destructive lately, so if you're here to usher me into life-threatening danger and intrigue, you picked a good day. You can start by telling me your name."

He said, "Happy birthday."

"With a name like that, you must have been teased in elementary school," I said. He smiled briefly and sucked the nicotine nipple. He wasn't such a bad guy, I mused. Probably just a misunderstood thug, cheated by the horrible things society has done to him. The glandular problem couldn't help. Maybe he'd come from a broken home, and is, thus, incapable of experiencing his emotions fully. I bet he's never been loved. I wanted to ask him what kind of women he sleeps with. Whether or not he pays for it. Perhaps he had a talent for juggling, or card tricks. I hadn't spent more than ten minutes at a time in the company of another human being in weeks. That order of loneliness can make people careless.

He said, "My boss told me not to tell you anything. Wants to tell you personally. If the money isn't good enough, then we can find another chick." I hadn't been called *chick* in a while. I dug it.

"My mother told me not to take candy from strangers," I said. "If your boss wants to talk to me, he can come down here himself. Or herself. But I'm not going anywhere for any amount of money until I know what this is about. OK, maybe for a million dollars, but no less."

The mountain immobile sighed, "The boss isn't going to like this."

Across the room, the office door clicked shut. I focused my peepers at the man leaning against it. He filled the room more than my smoking buddy, but he couldn't have weighed more than 165. He removed a cigarette from a black case and deftly lit it. The smoke curled over his tongue like a silk bathrobe. He had a tattoo—a dagger dipped in purple blood—on his left hand. I wondered if he had any more and where they might be. He said, "Wanda Mallory, P.I., owner of Do It Right Detectives. Home address, 115A Flatbush Avenue, Brooklyn. 130, 5'7". Twenty-eight, red hair, green eyes. Marital status," he smiled, "single."

"More like 127," I said, "first thing in the morning." He was the kind of man who could make me beg. He was trouble. I tried to get a take on him. He shifted his weight from one leg to the other, ready to pounce, run, or stand in the same spot for hours. Any of those options would be fine. He acted controlled, but willing to change gears on the highway. Worthy of fantasy and crammed with not-so-hidden charms. I wondered if he liked to go down.

"Are you the bank?" I asked.

He turned to the mountain, "Lars, wait outside. And take this." He handed over a gat the size of a small cannon. I was impressed. Lars took the heater and dutifully lumbered out without the slightest glance my way. The boss held up his arms and turned in a circle, keeping his eyes on me the whole time. He had an adorable rear end. "I don't have anything else on me," he said, "so there's nothing to be scared about." Some relief, I thought. The threat of a hidden arsenal was the least of my worries. He replaced Lars across from me in the client chair, moving quickly and easily. I got the idea that he knew how pleasant he was to watch. He shed his leather jacket.

"So," I said, leaning forward, "what do you know about me that you didn't learn at the DMV?"

"I know you might need some work. I know that you will do just about anything. And I know that you don't mind a little sweat."

"That depends who's sweating." A sudden flash: this guy, shirtless, after running ten blocks across town. "And you are?" I asked.

"The guy who's going to make you very happy."

"I've heard that before."

"But not from someone who means it." His voice was distinct only in its smoothness. No cigarette scrapes, although there probably should have been. I got the feeling that he's talked a lot, usually to convince, and hardly ever to insist.

"Look, babe, I can tell already you aren't going to make me anything but very, very sorry for talking to you at all." I paused. A flash: this guy on top of me, whispering the word *baby* over and over again in my ear. "But keep going," I said. "I like the way your mouth moves."

He smiled—a melter. In my high school years in New Jersey, I would have run in terror from a man this good-looking in the same way that men are reduced to babbling idiots when they meet truly beautiful women. There's a reason they're called stunners. I'd grown up plenty since then, but apparently not enough. My legs were clamped so tightly against my chair, they were beginning to throb.

He said, "Have you ever heard of Blood & Iron?"

"Motorcycle gang from the East Village."

"And have you ever heard of Strom Bismark?"

Strom Bismark was a downtown legend in New York City. He was the child genius/anti-Christ who started Blood & Iron at the tender age of sixteen. He took the gang from minor-league strip-down thievery, beatings, dismemberings, and recreational rape into the World Series of gambling, extortion— euphemistically known as *protection*—and, believe it, merchandising. Blood & Iron T-shirts for $25 a pop sold by the ton at their headquarters on East 11th Street. Bottle openers, cigarette cases, patches, and beer blankets were other popular items. Anyone who tried to hawk unofficial rip-offs on the corner would lose teeth and his choice of limb. No one tried.

B&I's appeal was mainly nostalgic—the brutality of the gang had, supposedly, lessened in the last five years or so. Now, a week didn't go by without a wet-kiss story in the newspaper about how some biker saved an old lady from being attacked. I don't know how the transition from outlaws to latter-day heroes mutated. Some downtown sociologists and journalists credited Strom's redirected passions. Instead of violence, he lusted for money. Bloodletting, lately, was his second string. Strom must have been over thirty by now. No one outside the gang really knew him well. It'd been theorized he hadn't left Manhattan island in the past fifteen years, much less the East Side. My ex-boyfriend and former colleague, Alex Beaudine, had a curious fascination with Blood & Iron. A vicarious thrill-seeker, that Alex. He didn't have near the nuts Strom must have had. Certainly not the nuts to fall in love.

My new visitor crushed out his cigarette in my ceramic amoeba ashtray. I said, "Yeah, I've heard of Strom Bismark. The scurvy dog—smitten so much with his own recidivistic nature that he probably can't piss in the toilet because it's the normal thing to do."

"Recidivistic? What's that?"

"You know, a habitual deviant, criminal. An example of societal ill."

He said, "It's a pleasure to meet you too." Of course. Charming as usual, Mallory.

"OK," I said. "You're the infamous Strom Bismark. Where are the severed heads, huh? Show me the ten little pigs you have tattooed on your butt for every woman you've raped." The legend, you see.

Strom said, "You don't really believe any of that, do you?" He looked at me in shock. "I've never raped a woman in my life." A crock or not, he had lovely sideburns. I'm into sideburns.

"Whoever you are, I don't mind sharing the same oxygen with you, but I'm a busy woman. I've got appointments. Lunch dates. You're holding me up." Strom surveyed the mess and then me. He knew I was full of it.

He said, "You really are a knockout."

I looked like shit. I hadn't showered that morning and my red mop frizzed out in angles nature never conceived. My wardrobe of the moment boasted a whole lot of nothing—Hanes men's T-shirt, too-tight jeans, and Vans.

I said, "Technical knockout?"

"On the floor with five cracked ribs."

I eyeballed him all over, but as a gams gal, I kept being drawn back to his legs. They were long and wiry in faded denim, ending in black combat boots. His left ankle rested on his right knee. Leaning back in the chair, he seemed relaxed and cocky, with long thin fingers stitched together over his belt buckle. His black T-shirt didn't hide a flat tummy, or the long taut arms of a guitar player or someone who's swung a whole bunch of axes. He was the knockout. I'd have to remember that he spoke for himself when he flattered others. A projector. I dimly remembered a Page Seven item on Strom in the *Daily Mirror* last year. There was no picture with the story.

I said, "Let's see some I.D."

"I don't have any."

"You ride a bike, don't you?"

"I don't have a license."

I said, "Got anything else?"

He pushed up his T-shirt sleeve, brandishing a tattoo that read "Leader of the Pack" stenciled across the Blood & Iron logo—a red-and-black leering bat, wings spread demonically. Anyone crazy enough to sport that who wasn't Strom would be long dead. He must be for real. I wished I could call Alex right away and tell him that Strom Bismark, *the* Strom Bismark, was right in front of me, chewing the fat in my office. But that was against my own rule: Alex and I were not permitted to contact each other for any reason as long as we live. A clean break. I thought it'd be easier.

Strom rolled down his sleeve and said, "I will pay you $500 a day. All you have to do is deal blackjack at my social club downtown. It's called the Outhouse. Maybe you've heard of it?" Strom's gaze wandered over my shoulder for a second, then back to me. "The hours are ten at night until five in the morning. You may have to readjust your internal clock."

"I'm a night person already." Strom's face: it wasn't what you would call conventionally attractive. His bones were too sharp, his skin too tight. He was almost too hard to be alive, except for the full red lips and the tornado behind his eyes. They were green, by the way. Like mine. We had so much in common. His hair was brown—a neat flat top. "How old are you?" I asked.

"Thirty-two. But I feel like I'm a hundred."

"You look it." But he didn't. He looked about twenty-five.

He said, "You're not very nice, Wanda Mallory."

"Don't take it personally."

He squinted at me for a second and then said, "I have nothing but good feelings about you."

"And I have warm gushy feelings for you, Strom. But I don't think we can work together. For one thing, blackjack isn't one of my games."

"What are your games?"

"Go fish." He didn't know if he should ask.

"OK. Straight up," he said. "A dealer of mine disappeared a week ago and I need a woman with your obvious charm and skills to take over for her while working undercover for me." A flash: Strom, lying naked in bed, a sheet straining across his hard-on, a bathrobe cord tied around his wrists. I hadn't been remotely interested in anyone since Alex left me. Then again, I'd barely gone out of the house.

"Obvious charms?" I asked.

He looked me straight in the tits. My nipples got hard. I crossed my arms over my chest—a mistake. "You'll fit the uniform," he said, "snuggly."

I paused, contemplating why it is that I blindly trust men I'm fiercely attracted to. He said, "What are you thinking?"

"That I forgot to buy milk." He blinked. I said, "Take it from the top. The whole story. And don't leave anything out, because I'll know."

His tattooed left hand traveled from his belt buckle to rub his neck. He hooked his right thumb under the waist of his pants, the remaining fingers grazing his privates. He said, "I'm not in a good financial situation. I'm closing in on bankruptcy for the gang and the club. Membership is down, and some personal business ventures of mine didn't work out as well as I'd hoped."

"What kind of ventures?"

"Just one, really. It's not important."

"It could be more important than you think."

"I know it's not important, and I don't like to talk about it." A vein pulsed on his neck. Strom seemed testy. This was obviously a sensitive spot. I could only imagine what this man would find disturbing.

"Go on. Chapter Twelve."

"I borrowed money from a friend and the deadline for payback is in a week."

"How much, from who?"

"A hundred grand."

"From who?"

"That's not important."

Strom had serious blockage. As a detective, it was my obligation to drain. I said, "I think we need to set up some rules. Just to make sure all runs smoothly and we don't lose our warm gushy feelings for each other. First, I ask questions. Second, you answer them honestly and cheerfully. Flamboyant hand gestures are optional, but completely appreciated. If you don't think you can do it, you'll have to buy someone else's time."

"I want to do this my way."

"Everyone does."

"I'll give you all the information you need as you need it."

"That and a token, my friend . . ." I said. Strom cocked one eyebrow, a neat trick.

He said, "Saint Nick gave me the money."

The joyous Christmas season died two weeks ago. With its last gasps went the Chia Pet commercials, bloated prices, and the city's sickeningly festive atmosphere. The day after New Year's, the street decorations came down and the Empire State Building switched off the green lights. Things had gotten back to normal and the people around town had remembered how much they hate each other. For girls like me, who take a shattered heart seriously, the post-holidays felt like a hot bath.

"Santa Claus gave you a hundred grand," I said. "You must have been a good boy last year."

"I mean Nick Vespucci. Loan shark. Everyone calls him Saint Nick." I never heard of him. Strom said, "He lent me the money last December. He expects to get it all back Sunday. The problem, as I said before, is that I don't have it."

"Interest?"

"No. We have an arrangement." I let that pass. For now.

"So why come to me? I can't whip together that kind of money. If you need a soufflé, then we can talk."

"I don't need you to make the money. I need you to find it. It was stolen from the office safe at the Outhouse." Strom leaned forward and seemed to study me like I was supposed to react in some specific way.

I shrugged and said, "Safecracking isn't one of my games either."

Strom's eyes clouded over, sending me anger vibes thicker than New York sirloin. "Maybe you have time to sit around all day with your thumb up your ass," he said, "but I don't. I came here looking for help, and if this is the price of admission, I won't pay shit." He deftly pocketed his cigarette case, slipped on his jacket, and stood up to go. And he was the most fun I'd had in weeks.

I said, "Leaving so soon?"

With the same angry monotone he said, "I never should have come to a woman in the first place. Especially one as lonely and hard-up for conversation

12

as you." Ouch. That hurt. Either Strom was intensely perceptive, or he had an innate ability to casually state people's worst fears about themselves.

I got down to business and said, "You came here for a reason, and if you aren't a complete idiot, you won't leave before you've explained yourself. So sit back down and spill your guts."

Before Strom could answer, Lars barreled in from the hallway. He said, "Crip on the bike phone." Bike phone? "He said it's urgent. Take this."

Strom took his gun from Lars and put on his jacket. He said to me, "Come now, or we won't see each other again."

I didn't have to think. I stood up, put on my coat, and was out the door.

The last time I'd ridden on the back of any motor machine was in junior high. It was a Honda moped. The guy who owned it—I can't remember his name— liked to show off by cutting quick turns that left skid marks on the cleanly mowed football field at the high school stadium. That was a night of many firsts for me. My first cigarette and my first ride on horsepower. And after ravaging the fifty-yard line marker, the nameless one whisked me off to Bobby Shohorn's front lawn a few miles away and gave me my first real kiss—with tongue and the requisite groping. It was summertime. He rode me home a few hours later when I wouldn't let him go to true second base (under the bra). I never kissed him again, but I thought about it all the time. When I told my girlfriends what happened—they'd all been kissed before—we agreed that nothing could possibly feel better.

But whizzing downtown on the back of Strom's Triumph—my arms gripping his waist, my thighs pressed against him—felt a whole lot better. At red lights, Strom rubbed his gloved hand on my leg, squeezing my muscle to relax me. It was freezing, but the heat from the machine rose up and warmed me all over. Twice, at jerky stops, I fell forward, my breasts bouncing into his back. He ignored it—he'd been bounced before.

We parked in the Blood & Iron illegally marked-off side of the street. Any civilian who dared to park there lived to regret it. One old story: a non-B&I biker, seeing all the other machines, left his there for less than an hour. He returned to find his bike disassembled to the last bolt, the pieces laid out in neat rows in the middle of the sidewalk. Few have made the mistake since. Strom hopped off the Triumph like he'd done it thousands of times, which, of course, he had. I kicked one leg over in what I thought to be a feminine, ladylike fashion only to burn my pants leg on the muffler.

Strom laughed. He said, "Every biker gal should have a muffler burn."

I fluffed my hair. My legs were still trembling. I asked, "What do you call it?"

"A muffler burn."

"No, I meant your bike." Naming treasured objects is as natural as naming children or pets. Like my gun—a pearl-handled .22 caliber revolver. You can't do a whole lot of damage with it, but people say the same thing about short-range missiles. I call it Mama. I named my spunky black she-cat Otis.

Strom said, "No one knows what I call my bike."

"So tell me."

Strom watched Lars pull up and park. Over the roar of his painfully predictable Harley hog (bike phone hidden in a compartment over the back wheel), Strom said, "You are the nosiest person I've ever met." I didn't know if I should feel insulted.

Lars, never graceful, dismounted his metal steed. He pointed to the man trotting toward us from across the street. Long and thin, he wore chaps, a cowboy hat, and a purple brocaded suede jacket, fringe strands dancing in the wind. He panted eagerly toward Strom, like a dog to its master. When he got closer, I noticed a semi-fresh scar that ran from his ear to his jaw.

His breath visible in the cold, he hollered, "We've got a doozy this time. I don't know what to do."

Strom said, "Calm down, Crip."

"Calm down, my ass. We got trouble big as Texas." His accent was thick and ridiculously fake.

"It can't be that bad," Strom said. "Let's take a look." We started across the street, presumably to the Outhouse. The buckaroo named Crip touched Strom on the arm.

"Hold on there," he said. "Who in the dang-blazes is this?" He pointed at me.

"She's my new girlfriend." Strom put his arm around me. It felt swell.

"Going for a new breed, huh Strom. I thought you liked your ladies younger than this filly. Girlfriend or not, she can't come see." Filly? I hated him already.

"She goes where I go." Crip moaned in protest. Lars, the silent-giant, tapped him on the shoulder and smiled. Crip grimaced.

He threw his fringed arms up in the air and said, "Fine, then. But if she comes over, she won't be your girlfriend for long."

We crossed East 11th Street to a brown building with pink fold-out shutters. On the ground level was an old Italian bakery/coffee shop with chocolate hearts in the window for Valentine's Day. I'd been there a few times. Great cannolis.

The Outhouse was on the second floor. One naked bulb lit the dingy stairway. It smelled like rotting wood. The door on top was unmarked. Crip pushed it open and we followed him through. The room, which took up the entire floor, was divided into sections. In one area, there were tables with wine-colored cloths, presumably for drinking and poker. The stocked-to-the-gills bar was off to the right, a full-size refrigerator next to it. There were three half-circle felt-covered tables in the remaining corners, all marked appropriately for blackjack. In the center was an oblong craps table and a roulette wheel. The walls were concealed by wine-colored drapes, and the ceiling fan couldn't dissipate the stench of the weekend's cigar smoke. The dimly lit salon lacked three things: clocks, mirrors, and windows. I understood this was usual for casinos, however puny.

Crip rushed us toward a door off the main room. CRIP BELUGA—MANAGER was painted on it in big, white block letters. EMPLOYEES ONLY underneath.

"Hang on to your hats," he said, swinging the office door open. I was behind Lars. His wooly mammoth frame filled the doorway and I could see nothing.

I heard Strom say, "Jesus Fucking H. Christ."

Crip said, "I just opened the door and ran out to call you. I didn't touch a thing."

Strom said, "Holy Jesus Fucking H. Christ." Lars didn't know what to do, so he continued to block me.

Crip said, "Trouble big as Texas. Like I told you."

Strom said, "Did you call the cops?"

"No chance, pardner. I was waiting for you."

"You moron. Call the goddam cops."

"This isn't exactly a legal establishment, Strom."

"The Chief of Police blew his Christmas bonus here last weekend."

Crip said, "Maybe if we pull a changeroo. The cops'd surely appreciate the effort."

Strom said, "Lars, move." Lars finally stepped away and I could see all.

She couldn't have been more than eighteen. I judged that not by her face, but by the untouched breasts which stuck straight up in the air. Her expression was tangled, locked in her last breath. The twisted, lifeless mouth said she hadn't died pleasantly. She had been beautiful. Around her head, on the once-cream carpet, was a hardened seepage of blood, spotted with chunks of gray streaming through her black hair. I'd never seen inside someone's skull before.

I felt sick but didn't want to turn away. I focused on Strom. His back toward me, he was on his knees near the body. He seemed to be looking for something. A weapon. Crip was leaning against the wall. He'd seen this already and had the dignity of a solitary first reaction. The second view turned his face green. He held one hand over his mouth. He snuck a glance at me. I surprised him visibly by not screaming, crying, or retching. I wanted to do all three, but for some reason, I couldn't figure out how.

Strom stood up, blood seeping through his jeans. He still had his back to me, and I wished I could see his face. He rested his hands on his hips and said, "There's nothing here."

Crip said, "I thought I'd seen the last of that girl."

I said, "Who was she?"

"Flush Royale," Strom said. "She's the runaway dealer you're replacing."

I mustered my courage and stepped into the room to look around, in effect, to mentally photograph the scene. Any detail could be important later. My eyes swept a 180. "Ah," I said, "a clue." I pointed to the wall in front of me. On either side of the doorway, letters in blood were splotched across the wall. I closed the office door to complete the message. It said: STROM BISMARK CAN SUCK MY DICK.

Crip said, "Well, I'll be hog-tied."

Strom said, "That's all I need."

I said, "At least we know the killer is a man."

CHAPTER TWO

A Matter of Splatter

Lust-worthy men are everywhere. Waiting on line at the ATM; sitting on stools in coffee shops; flipping through mysteries in bookstores. Herds of them ride the subway. I get glimpses. A thigh or a smile. Laser eye contact. If desire were a disease, New York should be a leper colony. The hundred or so times I've been tempted to say howdy to these young lovelies, I've hesitated. Three reasons: fear of rejection, fear of inadequacy, and fear plain-and-simple that the brute may be a hatchet murderer or, by some cruel twist, someone I owe money to. People say New York is a hard place to meet men. I would have to disagree. I see people fall in love all the time. True love does exist, but I don't think it exists for me. (Maestro, sound of a thousand tiny violins, please.)

Fancy finding myself surrounded by men, eyeing me expectantly and curiously, wondering if I was all I seemed. Most were young and virile and wore black shoes. If only I'd felt more like a bikini-clad homecoming princess sojourning to the winner's locker room and less like a criminal. I don't dig men in uniform anyway. Especially cops.

Among the swarm to descend on the Outhouse on that Tuesday afternoon were my old rivals Detectives Dick O'Flanehey and Tom "Bucky" Squirrely, the co-chiefs of homicide for the New York City Police Department. My dislike for the public dicks is perfectly mutual: they resent me for being a smart-aleck (female) P.I. who's done her share of showing them up. I'm indignant toward them for listing among their duties thwarting me or any other private dick in the name of pseudo-justice. To their credit, they hate to see a killer walk as much as I do.

Dick, as usual, had a Twinkie stuffed under his robber-baron mustache. When he saw me, he said, "Cupcake! Hanging out with a better crowd. Making new friends. I'm so pleased."

Bucky, nicknamed for his mutant overbite, said, "You tell her, Dick."

I was delighted to see them.

Before they'd arrived, the casino had been magically transformed into a lounge. The dice and roulette setups had been covered with Ping-Pong table planks, and wine-colored cloths hid the blackjack-marked felt. With the curtains pulled back, gray light from the windows washed away the sanguinary tone of the room. It was a welcome change. Strom told me that the Outhouse was designed for quick alterations as protection from surprise raids.

Detective Dick ran his show. He dispatched the uniforms to do the dirty work. They photographed the scene, dusted, chalked, and sealed. Strom, Crip, Lars, and I sat at one of the poker tables, smoking and waiting for the *Sturm und Drang*. I tried to assess my role there. I was my own gal, loyalties only to myself. Strom and Crip were obviously disturbed that the cops knew my name. Couldn't be helped. After a few minutes, I decided to play for Strom, even though my better judgment warned against it. Whatever my better judgment rules against is always worth a look.

The blue swarm buzzed around Flush in the office. I cared as much as the next innocent bystander when I happen across a cadaver. It's something you don't get used to, for more reasons than the smell. My sleuth curiosity wanted to know who she was and who killed her. I wondered if Strom would pay extra for a murder investigation. I wondered if I should get out while I still could.

The cops looked at me like they hated me. I reminded myself I hadn't done anything wrong. Finally, the men in white came. They removed Flush, which lifted a tension as weighty as the body bag. I let my shoulders relax and cracked my neck on both sides.

The uniforms filed out next. Dick, now alone with Bucky and us, took center stage. With aplomb, he said, "I'm tickled pink you called 911, Mister Bismark. Don't you usually take your bodies to Fresh Kills?" Fresh Kills is a landfill on Staten Island. It's the biggest and most toxic on the East Coast—a dubious distinction. "You get extra credit for doing the right thing, even if you are earthworm crap. I'd have to shoot you and then shoot myself if you ever touched my daughter. I guess we're all safe today," he said cheerfully. "I don't have a daughter."

Bucky added politely, "He's talking to the guys, Wanda."

"I gathered," I said.

"I could try and razz you until I spit blood, but I know you're not afraid of me. Cocksuckers, cocksuckers. I could put it to music and do a jig and you gentlemen wouldn't blink an eye." Dick twirled his mustache. He walked behind Strom. He was sitting with his arms crossed and his legs spread, with that same prepared-for-anything casualness I'd noticed earlier at Do It Right. Dick put his hands on Strom's shoulders and massaged. Strom tensed. "How are you, Mister Bismark? Feeling good?"

Strom said, "I've been better."

"I'm not so good myself."

"You don't look so good."

"I was just finishing my morning Danish when I got a call to check out a dead teenager. At the Outhouse no less. It gave me some indigestion."

"There's a drugstore around the corner," Strom said.

Bucky said, "That's real funny, tough guy." He was leaning on one of the neighboring tables. He found a toothpick in his pocket and jabbed away at his near-horizontal incisors. Dick and Bucky usually run the good-cop/bad-cop routine. At least they have with me. This time, and I think they knew it, it wouldn't work. To outlaws, cops are just mosquitos on butter, waiting to be swatted.

Dick said, "I see the situation this way: the killer knew you're closed Mondays and Tuesdays. But everyone knows that—even a badged, upstanding police officer like myself. He brought his young quarry here on an off day, when no one would be around. Got mad, got even, whatever. Hammered her on the skull with God knows what. Killed her. By that theory, he'd be an insider with access. That could be any of you.

"A B&E scenario, which I'm sure you like better, would be something like this. She was unfortunate enough to be nearby or inside during a burglary and she paid for it with her brains. He's quick with a battering ram, or whatever he used to smash that kid open. But why her? And why leave the message in blood? Who wants you to suck his dick, Strom, your boyfriend?"

Strom, eyes front, didn't respond for a few beats. "All I know is that I came back from a ride and found her. I called 911 to report the crime." He wasn't defiant at all. Just smooth as ice.

"As any model citizen would." Dick circled the table. "What about the rest of you? Same story, I bet."

Crip said, "Same as Strom. What he said."

I said, "Are we going to be arrested or not?"

"Late for the monthly henna?" That was Bucky.

Lars, tremendous in his silence, scraped grease from under his fingernails.

Dick sighed and said, "Seems like they've got their story straight. They must have prepared for us."

"Must have."

"Maybe we should change our strategy."

"The ol' Grease the Pipes routine?"

"Grease the Pipes, what's that?" Crip asked. "That doesn't sound wholesome."

"If you plan to use some kind of illegal coercion, I'll have to report you to the D.A." That was me. I try to sound official whenever I can. It impresses clients.

Dick said, "Shut up, cupcake."

He walked behind the chestnut wood bar. He ran his finger across the bottles. He said, "This is a beautiful bar, Strom. You must have some fun in this 'lounge.' Hell, let's loosen up. We've all had a bit of a shock." He came back and gingerly placed a gallon of mescal tequila in the center of our table.

"In some religions, death is a cause for celebration. A celebration of life." He plunked a shot glass in front of each of us. "So, as tribute to that poor stupid dead teenager, let's do this right and have ourselves a party."

"This can't be legal," Strom said.

"You drink for wrong answers," Bucky instructed. "We watch." Strom blinked. I made a mental note: at no point during the proceedings was I more convinced of Strom's innocence. He was weary, as we all were, from the horror of Flush's verité impression of road pizza. But, however stretched, he remained nonplussed. No doubt Strom would suffer the most from this death (after Flush)—the Outhouse would be closed down (and he'd be out much-needed bucks), he'd be staked out and brought in for questioning hourly, and he'd be perceived to have returned to his black-hat image. The selfless act of calling the police, willingly dumping himself into a pool of scrutiny when taking Flush to Fresh Kills, horrible I know, would have been easier, was reassuring. Maybe Strom Bismark really had changed.

Dick said, "First, I want you all to state your names and purpose for being here. Clockwise, Wanda go first."

"Wanda Mallory, girlfriend of Strom."

"Strom Bismark, lease holder."

"Crip Beluga, friend and colleague of Strom."

Lars didn't say anything. He poured himself a shot and downed it.

Dick and Bucky looked at each other and shrugged. Strom said, "Lars is a deaf mute. I'll have to answer for him. He's my bodyguard."

We'd started off badly. They knew Lars could talk. We drank. The method was a smart one, however college fraternity-like and barbaric. The loosest lips are tequila-soaked, and Dick and Bucky probably figured something would come of it. In short time, we'd gone through most of the bottle, incorrectly answering questions like: How many electrons are there in a carbon ion? What's the average yearly rainfall in Bangladesh? What's the gestation period for kangaroos? (a trick question—kangaroos being marsupials), and What color dress did Cher wear to the Academy Awards ceremony last year? (I knew that one—a fuchsia Bob Mackie creation. I drunkenly screamed the answer, to the surprise of my fellow questionees. I had to do two rounds for my lavish display.) Once we were all sufficiently sloppy, Dick and Bucky got around to the real business.

Dick said, "Who was she?"

"A nobody. She worked here." That was Strom.

"Nobodies don't get busted open like a watermelon."

"All I know is that I came back here from a long ride and found her on the floor." Strom teetered in his chair.

Dick said, "So you said. What do you know about her?"

"Nothing."

"That message to you. The killer must have thought her death would upset you. Even a score."

"My enemies are already dead."

Bucky, eager to get in on the action, turned to Crip, who was obviously reeling. He said, "You were her boss. Who was she? What was her name?"

Crip slurred, "She didn't know horseshit from blackjack when she showed up. But she sure knew how to lasso 'em in. Pretty little thing, did you notice? Long black hair. It's OK to say her name, right Strom? She went by Flush Royale."

Bucky said, "Any known family?"

Crip lollygagged, "I gotsta use the john."

"Answer the question."

"She was an orphan," Strom offered.

"Convenient. Did she have any enemies? She get herself in any trouble?"

Crip said, "She was a good girl. Never started nothing. She always talked about how good she looked, how good she felt. A happy thing, God bless her. She always said good this and good that. Good afternoon, Mr. Beluga. Good night, Mr. Beluga." He brushed a tear from his cheek. I couldn't tell if it was for Flush, death, show, or himself. "She was so young, and so sweet. So, what's the word?, pure and GOOD."

"So you're saying she was good?" I asked.

Crip swung his head toward me. He said, "Who in the dang-blazes are you?" He swung to Strom. "Who the hell is she?"

Strom put his hand on my cheek. It burned deliciously. When I leaned my head against it, he moved it away. He said, "I told you already. She's my woman."

Huge *pshaw* from Crip. "You'd never go for a gal like her. She doesn't even have any makeup on. She's so *normal.*" I was afraid he'd say plump. "Since when did you ever have a regular girl, anyhow?"

Strom sniffed and spit on the floor.

"And that name of hers—Wanda. I've heard it before. I heard someone talking about her. What kind of woman has cop friends? I'm telling you, she's somekinda snitch. Somekinda vixen, troublemaking snitch. She's got red hair like the devil and I don't care if she's steaming between the legs. Get rid of her. She's gonna blow the whole thing."

Strom said, "You're insulting my woman, Crip."

Bucky said, "Blow what whole thing?"

"Why don't you ask the snitch here?" said Crip. "I gotsta use the john."

Dick said, "What *are* you doing here, cupcake?"

I chirped, "I'm Strom's chick. Can't you see the kinetic love vibes flashing like lightning between us?"

"There's nothing between you two but air," observed Crip.

Dick twisted his mustache. Strom kept himself from strangling Crip. Crip gripped the side of the table for balance. Lars helped himself to another shot, downing it like water. Bucky started up again.

"How long did Flush work here?"

"I don't know," said Strom.

"Crip, you hired her."

Crip counted off on his fingers in slo-mo, missing most of the time. "Three months and two weeks. Three months and two weeks of pure joy and beauty."

"Correct me if I'm wrong, but I'm getting the feeling you had a thing for her." That was Dick.

"I got women crawling up my fire escape for a piece of this Texas pie." He cupped his package and shook, then groaned, remembering his full bladder. Humbly, Crip recanted, "She didn't want me, besides."

"How could she resist?" Bucky cracked.

Crip slurred, "There was one guy she liked. She smiled at him and leaned over him like this, showing off her cute round titties. Excuse me, ma'am." That was to me. "She sat in his lap and wriggled around like this, and when he got too excited he'd push her off and she'd giggle like a little girl for teasing him."

"You know him?"

"All I know is that my blood is turning yellar."

Dick said, "You notice a lot, don't you, Crip."

"I sure do. My mama down in Dallas always said that I've got an eye for seeing things."

27

"I've got two," I said. No one laughed.

"She's a funny one, for a vixen snitch."

"Tell us what else you saw," Dick prompted to Crip.

"She hung around after closing, some nights. I think she liked to nip at the hooch. And she was always writing notes to that boyfriend of hers."

Strom kicked Crip, under the table.

Crip yelled, "What? I'm not saying nothing. You hurt my dang leg."

Dick sighed and said, "No one knows, no one cares about poor dead Flush. Is that an accurate assessment of the situation?"

Crip, rubbing his bruised calf, said, "Ah, shucks. I cared about her. She had a wild streak, but it was just because she didn't know when to keep her mouth shut. But I cared about her."

"Then help us find her killer."

By-accident-on-purpose, Lars knocked over the mescal. It fell to the floor and shattered at his feet. On reflex, he jumped out of his chair (which for Lars was more like a heave), and elbowed Crip in the nose. Crip cried, "Oh, my nose." He grabbed his face and howled like a starved junkyard dog.

"I got a mind of my own, Strom," the urban cowboy blithered. "Don't forget that in a hurry."

I wasn't watching Crip at the time. I've found the truly salient information is usually in reaction, and not action. So, I kept my peepers on Strom. For the first time during the interrogation, he'd lost his smooth composure. His jaw muscles flexed and popped, and he rubbed his dagger tattoo so hard, it was like he wanted it to disappear. I wasn't sure what had happened or why Strom got so riled—my tequila goggles never stay on straight. Judging Strom's expression though, I gleaned much. Whether Crip had a mind at all remained to be seen. That he'd get a chance to prove it was not a safe bet.

The public dicks let us stumble down the stairs soon after. Whatever they were looking for, they must have found. It was colder than before. Even with my camel hair Donna Karan overcoat (sample sale, don't be impressed), I was freezing. That helped to sober me up. Strom beelined to the B&I headquarters across the street, Lars dragging Crip in tow. Strom wanted me to come, but I said I needed to talk to the cops. He said *fine* without a moment's hesitation and instructed me to hurry over when I finished. Dick and Bucky were taping a police seal on the Outhouse entrance when I approached them.

I said, "Hi, guys."

Dick said, "This is an ugly one, cupcake."

"I'm in."

"What's going on with you?"

"Strom hired me this morning. He lost something and wants me to find it." A wind rolled down the avenue and litter flew over the asphalt like tumbleweeds.

"I don't suppose you'd want to tell us what he lost."

"Sorry. Client confidentiality."

Bucky asked, "Why you?"

"Why me what?"

"Strom Bismark is one of the most powerful men on the East Side. He's got an army of mindless human machines who kill when he points a finger. He could have anyone and he wants you?"

"Hey, I've got a rep."

Dick guffawed. "Guys like him could give a flying fuck how many cheating husbands you've busted. Believe you me, cupcake, Strom Bismark does not consult the Yellow Pages. He's after something. We can help each other. Share information. This isn't about losing something, Mallory. A girl is dead and Strom must have been involved. Think about it. If you go alone, even money you'll end up on a slab."

"That's a nice thing to say to a woman you've just gotten plastered."

"He'll knock you down and you won't even see it coming."

He seemed genuine. I didn't trust it. I said, "Since when do you care what I do?"

"I care about Strom Bismark. The department has been after him for years. The last thing we need is some naive, infatuated dame P.I. to screw things up."

"Infatuated? I'd sooner kiss you." I lied.

"I hope you mean that, cupcake."

They got into their police vehicle. Bucky cranked down the passenger side window and said earnestly, "He's a liar, Mallory. Don't believe anything he says." With that advice, they sped up First Avenue, leaving me sloshed and shivering in the wind, full of dangerous ideas.

The Blood & Iron Headquarters building, once upon a time, had a red brick facade. The Strom/B&I era brought innovations to exterior building design through the modern medium of spray cans. The entire facade was covered—some enterprising biker thugs must have used a scaffold. The language reminded me of my New Jersey neighbor's treehouse: NO CIVILIANS ALLOWED, KEEP OUT OR SUFFER GRUESOME PUNISHMENT, TRESPASSERS WILL BE EATEN. Other themes included variations on SAVE A MOUSE—EAT A PUSSY. Lots of B&I logos. The colors were nice. The front door was red, like a big set of lips. I walked toward it when the light changed. As I got closer, the door creaked open. Lars was behind it. "Follow me," he said, and I did.

The inside boasted black walls and more graffiti, some of it over legitimate murals of bats and winged monsters from hell. A heavy chandelier hung from the ceiling. There were both a staircase and an elevator in back. Something was wrong. Even though twenty-odd bikes crowded the illegal lot, the headquarters was quiet, almost hushed, like a church. I asked Lars if Blood & Iron had all three floors. He nodded and gestured at me to turn left under an arch in the east wall. Painted on top of the arch was a likeness of Satan himself, adorned with a long blonde wig and fake eyelashes. A cigarette holder was perched between his clawlike fingers. He smiled smoke.

Quick digression: There are two kinds of people in the world—location people and non-location people. The former's personality changes depending on where she is. This supports the theory that places have souls just like humans and that a joint that makes location people uncomfortable has an evil squatter spirit. (I learned about that in the *New Age Journal*.) I'm not much of a discriminatory type. Everywhere I go is the same for me—any deviations depend on where I am in my monthly cycle. Deep in the headquarters' bowels, though, I wondered if I was getting more sensitive with age. For no good reason, I hated the joint.

We entered what Lars called a library but there wasn't a book in sight. The room was dark and vast and what someone from Long Island would think a haunted house looks like. There was an enormous desk and chairs on an Oriental rug. There was a chandelier on the ceiling, but it wasn't lit up. Sconces

31

with electric candles lined the one brick wall and two tall torchlights loomed behind the desk. The other walls were hidden by full-length drapes, obscuring any windows, like at the Outhouse. Lars told me to sit on what must have been a ten-foot-long couch with tassles on the sides. Red, of course. Red was everywhere. Lars propped himself in a corner and crossed his arms over his chest, like an Egyptian slave guard. I couldn't help glancing in the huge framed mirror on the brick wall opposite me. My skin seemed transparent and my hair stood up with static. I definitely had the creeps.

Strom strode in with a suitcase, his combat boots clumping across the floor. He sat behind the desk and grabbed the phone. He held up a finger to me and talked into the receiver without dialing. I was sure I hadn't heard it ring. He said, "I hope it's not a problem . . . You know how much I appreciate this . . . Of course I remember our talk . . . Fair enough." My head was swimmy from the ad hoc imbibing contest. The intense heat of the room didn't help. A radiator clanged somewhere, and my heart nearly flew up my throat. Strom hung up the phone and motioned me to him.

I didn't budge. "Where's Crip?" I asked.

Strom said, "He's puking in the bathroom. If you need to also, you can use the one upstairs."

"What the hell is going on here, Strom? You hired me to find your money and I wind up tripping over splattered girls."

"You don't have to worry about that."

"Well *you* better be worrying, because I'm not working for any cold-hearted biker fuck." I meant it. Strom knew her, and he was as cool as a zucchini. If a murder doesn't affect him, what would?

"I don't think I should have to prove how upset or not upset I am. Flush was someone I knew. I will deal with her death in my own way. I have trouble showing my emotions. Especially to women." He blinked. "And Wanda," he said, "don't take that personally."

I was sweating. The heat got too much so I slid off my Donna Karan. That felt better. I wanted to take off my sneaks but, no, that wouldn't be polite. I said, "Nice chandelier."

"We're waiting for an electrician."

"Twenty guys who can piece together a battalion of tanks can't fix a busted wire?"

"I never thought of it that way."

I asked, "How many bikers does it take to screw in a lightbulb?"

He said, "With a ladder, just one guy." He didn't get it. "Wanda, come over here. I want to give you something."

My pickled knees would have none of it. I said, "This couch sure is comfortable." He smiled. Then Strom and his legs sidled over and sat next to me. He placed the suitcase at my feet.

He said, "This is your uniform."

"I'm wearing luggage?"

"Inside. If you won't deal cards, the roulette wheel is the easiest thing to operate—I'll teach you. You start tomorrow night at ten. Meet me at the Outhouse office at nine. It'll be cleaned up by then."

"I'm not going to bother asking how you arranged all that."

"You must have other questions," he said, but stopped me before I could ask any. "Wait until tomorrow night." Strom leaned close and whispered, "You didn't say anything to the cops about the money?"

"Not a peep."

"I put your first and second day's pay in the suitcase." Strom touched my hair. He said, "I need you to do something for me. I need you to dye this black."

I flashed to the one time I quit smoking—a request from my boyfriend at the time. The first month was agony and I started up again immediately after we split. That's when I made the promise to myself. "No way," I said. "I won't change for any man."

"Only temporarily." I shook my head. He said, "It's part of your cover."

"Why black?"

"I adore it." I didn't respond. He said, "I'm not asking you to do anything criminal. You'll be the same person."

"But my hair. I love my hair." I sounded five years old—not the height of professionalism. "What about a wig?" I asked.

"Wigs fall off in bed," he said as smoothly as ever, which smashed my reluctance like a frying pan to the skull. A sudden flash: Strom and me in the bathtub together, washing each other's hair, black streaks running between my breasts. We are laughing.

He said, "I put a box of dye in the suitcase and a note. Be careful going home with all that money." A cue to split. I struggled back into my coat. Strom watched me and then gallantly kissed my fingertips, slowly on each hand, sucking gently on my pinkies. My knees got weaker. He raised his green eyes to meet mine and said, "You were beautiful today. I could get used to a woman like you." And then he left me. The word *sucker* rotated like sirens in my head. I ignored it.

Lars, my bovine savior, threw me and the suitcase

outside. I hailed a cab. On the ride back to Brooklyn, I realized what had been bothering me so much about that room: curtains shouldn't have shoes.

My apartment door in Park Slope was unlocked. I feared the worst, and that's what I got. Santina was stirring sauce, crooning "Summer Wind" and banging an olive oil bottle to the beat on the counter in my kitchen. My quadruped roommate, Otis, leapt at me when I came in, her claws lovingly extended. I dropped the suitcase on the floor with a thud to catch her, which scared Santina into kerplunking a wooden spoon into a pot full of tomato sauce. My kitchen walls were hungry anyway. She said, "Oh, it's you, thank God. My heart skipped twenty beats. You look revolting. I can't open this. Come over here and help me." She held out the olive oil.

I said, "Santina, what are you doing here?" As super for the building, she has a key. As my surrogate mother, she takes liberties.

"It's your birthday and I want you to be happy, is that too much to ask? That I make you happy? Cook you a hot dinner? Talk your blues away? If it is, I'll go. I'm not hurt. You haven't let me near you for weeks. I'm not insulted. What do I know, if you want to be miserable, be miserable." She's an OK cook, but she's a guilt gourmet.

"I'm happy, all right? I'm happy as a pig in shit." I'd plumb forgotten my birthday.

"Language like that is very unbecoming, Wanda. You'll never attract the right kind of man with that gutter mouth of yours." She sampled her sauce and made yummy sounds. "Get your butt over here and taste this. I can't stand myself, I'm so brilliant with oregano." Santina Epstein is a fiftyish, half-Italian,

half-Jewish beautician. She works at the Adrienne
Argola salon on the Upper East Side, transforming
rich old ladies' straw-hair into spun gold. Her own
hair is a blonde (fake) beehive, and she dresses better
than her hoity-toity clients. She's an ex-confirmed
bachelorette, only recently engaged to her live-in
boyfriend, Shlomo Zambini. He's a doctor. They met
at the emergency room at Mt. Sinai when she got an
infected hangnail from a botched manicure. But that's
another story.

I dropped Otis on the floor and crossed the
furniture-deprived living room into my walk-through
kitchen. When I got close enough, Santina said, "God,
you stink to high heaven."

"Job hazard." She scowled. She hates that I'm a
gun-toting gumshoe and would rather see me gnawing
on pencils in law school than eating lead. I tasted the
sauce and it was divine. I remembered that I was
hungry. It was after three.

My apartment, big by Manhattan standards, is
average for Brooklyn. The twelve-foot ceilings and
wood floors are what make the place a find. It's a
railroad—all the rooms are off a long hallway, including my bathroom with tub, and my bedroom, dubbed
by a particularly enthused ex-boyfriend as the Love
Cove. The whole joint is usually pretty untidy (another ex said it looked like I was always on the verge of
moving out), but that's how Otis and I like it. When
she gets the chance, Santina sneaks down from her
place upstairs and straightens. I've tried to stop her,
but she says, "What, you think I want your roaches?"
and I shut up. With her, it's always easier to shut up.

I figured a shower and change would do me right, so
I adjourned to the bathroom. The water was hot and
steamy. It helped wash away the tequila smell and

midday hangover, but not the ongoing Strom fantasies. Desire—I think about it sometimes and get scared. The lust generating in my little body alone could light Baghdad. I stepped out of the shower and wiped a hole in the steam to check my look in the mirror. Not bad. A new interest always pumped fire through my flesh. And I seemed thinner—always a good thing. I hadn't spent much time in front of mirrors lately. My vanity came in waves.

I wrapped one towel around my waist and another turban-style on my head. Santina was sitting on my bed when I came out. She held up what must have been my new uniform—black leather miniskirt, side zipper, and bustier. The fishnet stocking lay shriveled across her lap. She'd done it again and rummaged through my personal things. I was too tired to fight about it.

"The instructions suggest black pumps," she said.

"What do you think? My Joan & David's?"

"This is vulgar and putrid," she said, flinging the outfit behind her. "Nice men, lawyers, bankers, doctors, they like cotton and linen. Even better, silk. This leather stuff is not for you. I know."

"It's Gaultier inspired, Santi. Very now. Very happening."

She clucked disgust. "I don't like this one tiny bit. What kind of lowlife, sleazeball gave you this anyway?"

"No one special. Just some outlaw biker. He's pretty hot too."

She squinted at me. She couldn't tell if I was lying. She said, "Look, Ms. Tough-as-Rawhide, don't you yank my chain. I've got enough problems of my own, what with you risking life and limb, holing up in that revolting snakepit of an office in Times Square. I worry about you. You're vulnerable; you've been hurt. You might fall into something you can't handle." She showed her teeth. "I could kill that Alex . . ."

"Santina, shut up now or I swear I'll have to hurt you."

"And this," she clucked while picking the box of Miss Clairol from the suitcase. She held it with two fingers like it was fish paper. "Use this and it'll look like someone lacquered your head. You touch your hair and I'll kill you. Such natural beauty—look at you. Millions of depressed women come into Argola and demand that color red." She flung the box in the trash across the room. It went in, two points.

"Black is more dramatic."

"You're dramatic enough. You carry a gun, for Christ's sake. But," she relented, "if you're going to do it, let me do it properly. Listen to me, are you listening? I'll go to the store and pick something up. My birthday gift to you. We'll have fun. Eat, talk, dye. You want to be a slut, I'll make you look seedier than a pomegranate."

"That'd be groovy," I said. I gave her a hard time, but Santina, pain in the ass, always comes through in the clutch. She ran out, jumpy with a new purpose, energized to be needed. She'd put me through no battle, no wrench-to-the-throat subtle persuasion. It was so unlike her.

Alone at last. It felt familiar. I pressed the tiny scraps of leather across my chest and hips. Snug, as Strom predicted, was right. The fishnet stockings depressed me deeply. I'd have to shave every day—not my style. I lay down on the bed and closed my eyes. I fell asleep and dreamt about the Ferris wheel at Coney Island.

* * *

"Things I don't understand disturb me," Santina espoused while pushing my head under the bathroom sink faucet. "Computers, cellular phones, digital ovens. And you, Wanda, you disturb me." Black trails of dye streamed down my cheeks. "This detective garbage. What's the attraction? What good is there in it? You're broke all the time, you're lonely. You don't meet nice people. And then there's that whole Alex disaster."

"It's getting in my eye."

"I met a nice young man the other day. He came in with his grandmother, poor woman, loses fifty million more hairs every time I see her. So anyway, I said to him, I said 'Have I got a girl for you.' I told him all about you and he got very excited. I gave him your phone number."

"You what?"

"He's an investment banker. Bear, Stearns. Cuter than a bug's rear end, trust me." Trusting Santina is like dancing naked at a prison rodeo. Not a good idea.

I said, "If he calls at all, it's probably because you painted me as an easy lay."

"Aren't you?"

"No. I'm not. Why is the woman always the easy one, anyway? Guys are easy. Just brush their arm with a tit and they convulse on the floor."

"That's because they're buckets of overflowing hormones."

"Then why aren't they our slaves?"

She handed me a towel. "Fluff." I fluffed.

"Did it take?" She'd used Preference by L'Oréal—raven black.

"It took. You look like Morticia Addams. It's still wet. Don't touch." I followed her into the kitchen.

She stuck her head in the oven to check the lasagna. It smelled luscious as a full-body rub. I sat at one of the bar stools around the butcher-block island in my kitchen. I lit a cigarette.

She tested to see if dinner was ready. I said, "I'm not dating this loser."

"So don't date him. Like I care? He's a nice boy, I gave him your number. So maybe you go out, have a good time? See more of each other, hop in the sack, make each other happy, whatever. Life is hard enough, right? You don't need me helping you."

"That's right, I don't."

"You don't need anyone."

"Otis is nice."

"So do what you want. You always do anyway. Like I care if you're lonely and depressed? What do I know? Be miserable." She pulled the tray out of the oven and cut into the noodles. "I'm only giving you a little slice. That butt of yours." She blew out her cheeks.

I took a long drag. Santina gets cozy in her ruts. She lies down flat and refuses to budge. A few months ago, all she wanted was for me to go to law school. That being completely out of the question, the harangue didn't bother me. This dating rampage, this bothered me. I desperately wanted to change the subject. I said, "What do you know about roulette?"

"David Niven."

"A little ball on a big wheel, we are speaking the same language?"

"David Niven was in some movie, some gambling movie. Or maybe it was Gary Cooper. Anyway, he was dressed like all get-out—tuxedo, beautiful patent leather shoes. I'd toss Shlomo in a millisecond for a man like that. Can you stand me? I'm so fickle."

"The game, Santina."

"The higher the risk, the bigger the payoff. And the bigger chance of losing. It's best to go with light bets. Black, red, odd, even. You, Ms. Nit-Picky Smarty Pants, only go for high-risk bets—guys who do not understand the meaning of the phrase *emotional commitment*. And that, my dear, is why men are not your slaves." She fingered a clump of sauce and licked. "So, you'll lose every time," she said. "The wheel's designed that way."

"People win."

"On low-risk bets. Like that nice banker boy."

"I'd rather go dateless forever than be that boring."

She said, "Don't say that. Don't even think it. And that boy is not boring. He's just not an animal, like most of the guys you go out with."

"Alex was no animal." Except in the hopper.

"Alex was dog meat. He got you in and didn't help you get out."

"He was a perfect boyfriend."

"Perfect boyfriends don't leave," she said in a moment of brutal clarity. I digested that and put out my cigarette.

Santina pushed a minuscule wedge of lasagna at me—my birthday portion. I took down the hair turban. "Your hair looks horrible," she consoled. "Eat."

CHAPTER THREE

It's Halloween Every Night in the East Village

Flush Royale must have been of the deeply vexing breed who look good in clothes and better out of them. Having seen her half out of them, I was sure of the latter. I squirmed into her tartwear ensemble and decided I must be the type who looks best in skin (a nice rationalization). My pliant flesh loathes constraints—especially leather ones. Leather doesn't breathe. After zipping up the mini, neither could I.

But I loved my new hair. Talk about change. Red hair is so obvious; I'd always stuck out like white bread at a Bar Mitzvah. Now I could move easily, blend in, be as absent as any brunette, and I relished the chance. Anonymity, like a driver's license, is a privilege, not a right. With my raven locks, I'd finally earned that privilege.

I hung my fuzzy overcoat over my outfit and clicked down Flatbush Avenue to the subway in my pumps. The air was still cold and there weren't many people on the street. It was 8:00 P.M. on Wednesday night. It wouldn't take me an hour to get to the Outhouse, but there was detecting to be done. A half-hour of covert surveillance couldn't hurt.

It bothered me that I couldn't remember what the story about Strom was in the *Mirror* last year. And I live for Page Seven. I'd spent the afternoon at the Brooklyn Public Library, a pleasant stroll up Flatbush from my apartment, and hunted for all the clippings I could find on Strom and Blood & Iron. The pile of Xeroxes could have choked a water buffalo. I didn't have time to go through it—dolling myself up had consumed the evening hours. Just getting eyeliner on right took hours.

I hopped the 2 train at Bergen Street and changed for the Lex line at Nevins. The ride into Manhattan was uneventful, except for one bizarre voyeuristic moment. I was sitting next to a woman when a babelike guy boarded the train and stood right in front of us. His wallet was dangerously visible in his front pants pocket. I was staring at it, thinking how easily I could lift it. No sooner had the thought rotated around my brain when the woman, young, pretty, secretaryish (big blonde hair), stood abruptly and flirtatiously bumped into the man. She apologized way too profusely, especially considering that brushing up against hard male bods is de rigueur for boring subway rides. He smiled at her and forgave her clumsiness. She got off at the next stop, and when I turned again to look at the man's hips at eye level, the wallet was gone. I chuckled to myself, and silently applauded the woman. She wasn't smooth, no, but she'd been slick. When I got off at Union Square, the man, still grinning from the contact with a pretty woman, didn't know what had happened to him. Men are such idiots. (I'm not bitter . . . much.)

I headed downtown in the cold. The streets were covered with filth, both inanimate and near-animate. Even in my overcoat and new hair, slimes made those revolting clucking, kissing sounds as I walked toward the Outhouse. I was so flattered I wanted to puke. I positioned myself against a street sign at the northwest corner of 11th and 1st, across from one of the Polish kielbasa joints in the nabe. The headquarters was southwest, the Outhouse southeast. The traffic lights flashed green and red on the slick black pavement. I put on my glasses, lit a cigarette, shivered, and waited. At five to nine, Strom left B&I and ran over to the club. I'd never seen him run, outside my fantasies. His stride was long and elegant. I remembered what Dick and Bucky said about not trusting him. That wouldn't be a problem. I don't trust many people. I wondered if trust was necessary to get in bed with someone and then decided it wasn't. Sex requires only desire, and sometimes not even that. Sex with Alex had been easy. So easy, in fact, that I couldn't say it was worth the effort. There was no effort. It just happened all the time. I checked the time—9:07 P.M. I was late: how time flies when one's mind turns to bodies. I crossed the street and went up. I made myself stop thinking about sex.

That became impossible. When he saw me, Strom said, "Your hair is beautiful, Wanda. Take off your coat." We were in Crip's office. The carpet had been cleaned, but a dark shadow remained where Flush's squashed cranium had been. The message on the wall had been painted over. When Strom gave me the twice over, I got chills. I felt more like I'd arrived at a date than a job.

Strom looked hot as a chili pepper. He wore his combat boots, black Chinos, and a white T, sleeves cut at the shoulder. I noticed for the first time that his chest was hairless. I took off my coat and Strom rewarded my evening efforts with a low whistle. He

44

walked toward me and said, "You're everything I imagined." He took a tendril of my hair in his hand, held it to his nose, and sniffed. He smiled and spun me around to see all angles. "The glasses have to go. Otherwise, babe, you're perfect." A flash: Strom and me, naked but draped in chinchilla, flinging champagne flutes into the ski lodge fireplace in Gstaad. A fluffy image—not one of my usual oozing fantasies. Zsa Zsa had been getting too much press.

"Strom," I said, "murder first."

"I've been talking to cops all day long. I need a break. We can talk later." He traced a finger along the top of my lace-up bustier.

"We can talk now," I said. His tattooed hand brushed over my breasts. Even through leather, it burned.

"Let's not talk," he whispered in my ear before he kissed me. I tried to focus on the conversation.

"Who killed Flush, and why? And don't pretend you don't know."

"Wanda, we already discussed this. I don't know, and it doesn't concern you." Strom leaned into me, full body smush. "Forget about it."

"I can't do that."

"Let's find the money first." He encircled my wrists and wrapped my arms around him. His eyes traveled lazily from my mouth to my eyes and back again. I found this distracting—his desired effect. To stop my questions, or excite me?—I couldn't tell. I struggled not to respond. Had I mentioned that I hadn't had sex in months?

"Strom, honey, are you protecting someone?"

He pressed eagerly into my hip and unzipped my mini. He seemed puzzled that it didn't fall to the floor. (Yes, it was that tight.) We were standing where

Flush's leaky corpse lay a day ago. This was not a turn-on. I untangled myself, sucked in, and zipped up. He sighed and walked behind the desk to sit. He said, "I haven't been turned down in a long time, Wanda. I know, I know. I won't take it personally."

"I like you plenty, Strom. And if the indentation in my hip is any indication of how you feel about me, I'd say we like each other."

"You like me, and you're pushing me away? That could make some guys awful confused, Wanda. Some guys might even get mad." That I already knew; I went to Dartmouth.

"Mad enough to kill?" I asked. "Might that move someone to splatter gray matter with an unidentified blunt object?" No murder weapon had been found. I read that in the morning edition of the *Mirror*.

"I'm talking about sex, Wanda. Not murder."

"Both subjects are equally frustrating. Come on, Strom. Help me out here. About the money. About Flush. The meter's running."

"Let me show you the wheel. I promise we'll talk later." And he dragged me into the casino. I left my Donna Karan and Mama in the office—Strom said they'd be safe. I tried to measure to what depth he'd manipulated me by flirting so shamelessly. He'd succeeded all right—I didn't ask him another question before he ran off (business, he said). But why Strom was being so evasive, I hadn't the slightest. Patience, my old enemy, was in his corner. It appeared to be a fight to the death.

"What in the dang-blazes do you think you're doing?" Crip blithered after I'd made my hundredth mistake as roulette caddy. His nose was a stunning shade of purple from Lars' elbow jab the day before. I

46

had a strange desire to squeeze it. "You roll the dang ball in the opposite direction as the wheel. Shee-it."

"That contradicts my basic linear nature, Crip."

"Contradict this, darlin'," he said, cupping his package. The Outhouse opened at ten and about a dozen people came in. Blackjack was the game of choice, and the action at the wheel wasn't so hot. The game is much more complex than I thought. Every player used a different color chip and every bet pays differently, based on the odds. One can bet on a whole row of numbers, which didn't even occur to me. And the player can't lay his money down until the ball is rolling. This results in much frenzied activity. From my side of the table, it was plain chaos.

I did have help. A pudgy fellow in a cheap suit sat on a stool to my right. His hair was clean, but mangled. He was the odds man. He wielded his pocket calculator like a ginsu knife and had every bet tabulated before I'd even registered what slot the ball had fallen into. (Strom'd made me take off my glasses.) His name was Billy and he incessantly hummed a lunar tune. I'd never heard it before. Apparently, Billy was some variety of autistic savant, or that's how Crip explained him to me. I didn't think that was it, even though he never made eye contact and never spoke. My guess was that he had all his mental and emotional resources, but chose not to use them. He must have been abused in some way, badly enough to have retreated from human contact.

I began to feel for him, so I tried to press him for a response by asking how old he was. He punched numbers into his calculator, rotated it in his hand, and held it inches from my face. It read: hI LOIS which was really 5107.14 upside down. I asked him where he lived. He punched furiously. The message this time said ShELL.OIL (710.77345). I asked him if this was the only way he communicated. He punched up BIG.BOOBS (58008.918). I told him to shut the fuck up.

Gambling types are not gentlemen. Even though one spin of the wheel took all of five seconds, the piggish clientele found time to make unsavory comments about my wardrobe. And I was beyond uncoordinated, dropping the ball, accidentally scattering chips. I was so busy making a fool of myself that I couldn't learn anything about anyone, let alone the man who'd hired me. On top of that, my heels were executing the death pinch on my big toes. I was on the verge of splitting when Crip rescued me.

He called to a woman in my outfit working the bar. "Crutch, get your candy-ass over here." She dutifully hobbled over—her heels made mine look like dress-up rejects from kindergarten. I'd guess she was twenty-five and at least six feet tall. Whatever sand she was missing on top was compensated by her ample posterior. I'd always thought men liked hard, petite butts. But when Crutch glided passed, every guy in the joint sighed as if drugged by the motion of her cheeks. They rolled like two cats fighting in a bag. She seemed friendly and sweet and obviously had something going with Crip. I knew this, because he was the only man in the place she'd look in the eye.

"You," Crip snarled to me. "Get into my office." I followed him in, happy to be saved and hoping I'd get some information about Flush and the missing money.

Once in the private room, Crip sat down and said, "Tell me true, darlin'. You're no more Strom's gal than I am." There was no chair for me, so I teetered.

I said, "Were you in love with Flush?"

"Shoot. I love all women."

"How'd you get the scar?" He ran a finger along the mark from his chin to his ear. It was week-old fresh.

"Childhood accident. My momma dropped a skillet. She didn't mean nothing. That woman's heart is big as Texas."

"So where do you come from?"

"From my dick. You?"

"I've heard better Texas accents on parakeets."

"Then you must know some pretty impressive parakeets, sugar."

This was going nowhere. I decided to test Crip's loyalty. "Strom was mean to you yesterday," I said. "I hated watching that."

He puckered his lips, weighing my words. "Strom is an emotional man," he said, "underneath."

"He's dreamy." I meant it.

"Magic exists on this earth, darlin'. It grows in some people. Strom's like that. He's got whatever it is that makes other people do things for him. Things they normally wouldn't do. If I were you, sugar, I'd think twice before doing anything for him, or asking questions that might get back and upset him."

"Is that what Flush did? Upset him through you?"

He puckered again and neurotically ran his finger over his scar. He said, "If you kick one crutch from a cripple, he'll just reach for another. I'm always reaching."

"Thank you for sharing, but it doesn't answer the question."

"You're like that too, I reckon."

"I always answer questions."

"I meant replacing one love with another. How's that busted heart of yours doing, anyhow?" We'd suddenly boarded the Concorde to the Twilight Zone.

He laughed at my surprise. "I figured out who you are," he said. "And I don't like you. Far as I'm concerned, you got Flush killed." My head spun. I thought frantically for a connection.

"Try not to look so guilty, darlin'."

Suddenly, we heard a crash from the casino. A woman screamed. Crip and I ran out to see what was happening. The roulette table was turned on its side like a lassoed heifer, the wheel in pieces on the ground, chips everywhere. Crutch stood in the center of the room, crying with her hands over her face. All the gamblers and other dealers were pressed against the drapes, cowering in fear. The cause: a tall, thin man with long, brown hair and a leather jacket, on his knees, pounding both fists on the floor like a lunatic. His hands were splintered and bloody.

Crip yelled, "Hey, cowboy, what the hell do you think you're doing?" He trotted over and pulled the man to his feet. The man squinted at Crip, cocked his arm back and slammed him in the jaw like a jack-hammer. Crip made a nice sound when he got hit, the suede jacket muting a loud thud. The man planted his sneaker on Crip's neck and said, "I know you did it, you stinking piece of barbecued Texas cowmeat." Crip begged and pleaded. Finally, he wriggled free and crawled over to the bar. The man watched motionlessly. He looked at his bloody hands in disbelief and turned slowly toward me. His eyes were wild, and they got worse when recognition set in. My hair. No wonder. "This is Flush's boyfriend," wheezed Crip, the human punching bag. "I think you've met already."

The man mouthed, "Wanda?"

"Alex," I said. "Nice jacket." In past winters, he'd always worn his wool blue-and-gold Michigan varsity.

Letter in track. He never let me wear it outside. This leather number was my six-month anniversary gift to him. We broke up before it got cold enough to wear.

Alex stepped toward me. When he was close enough, he tried to hold me. I snapped. "Don't you dare touch me." That hurt him, I could tell. He turned his back on me. Again.

The wild man I saw that day was not the gentle hamster of a boyfriend I'd practically lived with for a year. The three months since our finale must have changed him. Or maybe he'd had a bad day. Maybe I never really knew him. I realize that's something everyone says when they get dumped. That, and I never really loved him. Whatever. In my case, only the former applied.

The day Alex and I ended it, I had the flu. It was mid-October, and we'd spent the past two weeks chasing after the wayward husband of a young, beautiful Wall Street wife named Penelope Bradshaw. She and her husband, Winston, had gotten married fresh out of Bowdoin. He proceeded to get his MBA at Columbia while she, a political science major, worked as a temp for the Cosmopolitan Agency. Once he got a job at Whitestone and Little, she stopped working altogether and focused her attention completely on him and transforming their Park Avenue cooperative into a showplace. She swore to us when she first came to Do It Right that she still adored Winston after eight years of marriage. She loved their friends and her co-op.

Alex asked her, "So what do you need from us?"

On that, she burst into tears and showed us the letter. She said it was in his handwriting and that she found it inside one of his suit jacket pockets. It read:

51

"It's been days and all I can think about is the smell of you. It is uniquely you and so mind-numbing that I wish I'd never gotten close enough to taste you. If we don't see each other again soon, if I can't bury myself between your legs soon, meaning this week, I'll go out of my mind. So now you know you've got me. I relinquish control. It's funny to think that when we started up, I thought you'd come begging for me. I should have known." And that was it. No signature, no address.

Alex suggested to Penelope that Winston had written the letter for her. She said, "The smell of me? I wear Joy by Patou. I smell like every single one of my friends. Unique? Mind-numbing? Please."

Alex curled his lips and said, "I don't think he was talking about the smell of your neck." She blushed from her collarbone to her temples, like cherry syrup sucked up a straw.

"If you mean what I think you mean," she said, "he's never done that for me. I've asked him, but he refused every time. So he wouldn't know what I smell like."

I took a good look at Penelope Bradshaw and visions of the virgin-whore phenom punched their way into my thoughts. She was petite, expensively dressed, scrubbed and rosy like she showered five times a day. She was virginal—and I don't mean that to be insulting. I couldn't imagine that there were still men out there who thought that marrying types are not meant for experimental sex, or that going down on a woman was anything but a prerequisite for intercourse, anyway. That a man would deprive his wife her pleasure and save his sexual daring only for his mistress was beyond bad judgment and rode in tandem with the kind of misogyny I learned about in

Women's Studies courses in college. That alone infuriated me. Also, I should mention that I was deeply in love with Alex at the time, and watching Penelope react to the evidence of her husband's betrayal swept a sympathetic pang through my heart. The thought of Alex touching another woman, or doing something for her he wouldn't do for me, was paralyzing. The only thing he wouldn't do was take baths with me. I don't know why.

My flu began to kick in within a week of Penelope's first visit. By that time, we'd managed to locate Winston's rendezvous spot, a loft building in Soho, but we had yet to get details on the woman in question. Every time Winston went there (about twice a week), a Chinese delivery boy came within an hour of his arrival. We couldn't be sure that Winston'd ordered the food, obviously, but in one of Penelope's crying jags about how magical he was, she told us that Chinese was his favorite. Our plan of action: I'd pay off the delivery boy and Alex'd take his place. When Winston, or the woman, answered the door, Alex would take the delivery into the kitchen and shoot everything and everyone he came near with his trick lapel camera—the shutter release connected to a wire tucked into his coat pocket. It was a lame plan, but my fever was reaching 102 degrees. I was near death and couldn't wait for a better idea.

Also, the case had become a personal thing. The male betrayal had seeped into my system as ferociously as the flu, and I started to picture every woman on the street lathering up in the tub with Alex. Rationally, I blamed my hallucinations on the sickness. But for the sake of my health, sanity, and relationship, I had to wrap the case as soon as possible. Thus, the lameness of our plan.

The Flu God rescued me that night. Alex managed to get pictures of Winston in his boxers (blue stripes) and his mistress in lingerie (black teddy). She was an older woman. We called Penelope in, and when she saw the photos, she fainted. She came to in a few minutes and cried for an hour. Through her gulps, she got out that the woman—the mistress/whore—was, in fact, her mother. She'd always found it strange how willing Winston was to have dinner with the in-laws. Then her memory kicked in, and she flashed to the wedding picture of Winston and her mother dancing, his hand on her hip just so; the time she'd found them embracing in her Park Avenue kitchen when they were supposed to be pitting avocados; how wet with nervous sweat the receiver was whenever Winston passed the phone to her after perfunctory conversations with his mother-in-law. She said she felt like a worthless idiot, that she should have known.

She took our pictures. We took her money. It's a sobering feeling, getting paid to ruin people's lives. She turned down our consultory dinner invitation, insisting she'd be all right, and closed the door behind her. I probably would have cried for her, but with the dehydration from my fever, I didn't have the water in me.

Alex and I took a cab to my apartment in Brooklyn. He was more or less living with me at the time. After I fed Otis some Liver Puree, Alex suggested I get in the tub. I might feel better; he'd read in the living room, no problem. I didn't notice how distant he was. I'd been too distracted by the case and by my flu to see his impatience with me. Or realize I hadn't paid any attention to him the whole time. All I could think about was my own misery. (Santina would say I was blaming myself again—that it was not my fault. That he should have been paying more attention to me. I was sick; I was freaking out about the case. I obviously was going through a hard time. He should have been grateful I didn't die from my fever. And so on.) I told him a bath sounded great, but only if he'd join me.

"Can we not do this right now?" he asked.

"Do what?"

"This argument upsets both of us, and I'm too tired to have it."

"I wouldn't want to put you out."

"For the hundredth time, Wanda, sitting naked in hot water makes me feel like a soft-boiled egg."

"Goddam it, Alex, the devil's hands have been sticking out of the ground and grabbing at my ankles for days. I could use a little support. I could use a little affection. I feel like I'm going to snap." I pounded my knees. "Heart of my heart," I ranted, "if you don't do this for me, I don't think that we should go on."

"Go on where?"

"Go on at all."

"So basically," he said calmly, "if I love you, I should take a bath with you, even if I have a personal detestation for the activity?"

"Yes."

"You're being . . ."

"Don't try to tell me I'm being unreasonable, overly emotional, or manipulative. I hate those words."

"You're sick and tired and grouchy. So am I. This case was rough for me too. I know I'm not seeing clearly right now. And I don't think you are, either. So let's just hold off until tomorrow."

"I'm seeing clearly for the first time all week. And what I'm seeing is that if you don't take a bath with me, our relationship isn't worth sand in the desert."

He stared at me, sweaty, red, and angry on the bed.

Finally he said, "Let's get it over with," and took off his shirt. The bath lasted all of five minutes, half as long as it took to run the water. Our legs couldn't help touching, but other than that, he stayed as far away from me as possible. He didn't want to catch anything.

That night, in bed, I couldn't sleep. I was burning up and angry at Alex for turning his back to me. We'd always slept tangled up like kittens. I moved over to him and dangled my arm over his waist. No response. I looked to see if his eyes were open. They weren't. I kissed his back and rubbed against him. He stirred and gently touched my thigh. He said, "I'm asleep, honey. Is it OK if we wait until tomorrow?"

"No."

"Tomorrow morning. I promise. I'm too tired right now."

I turned him to face me. "What is this tomorrow shit?"

"Here we go," he sighed.

"You don't really love me, do you?"

"Wanda, what are you doing?"

"You don't love me."

"I took a bath."

"But you don't really love me."

"And I would if I fucked you?"

"Yes."

"So if I don't fuck you this very second, it means I don't love you?"

"Yes."

"Do you realize how ridiculous that sounds?"

"You obviously don't understand me."

"What if I said that to you? You'd hit me and walk out."

"I would not."

"You would too. Now please, Wanda, it's late. I've had enough of this for one day."

"I'm sleeping on the couch." I rolled away and sprang out of bed. Unfortunately, my spine stayed behind. A flu will do that to you. I fell back next to him. He held me and kissed my shoulders. He said, "Is it OK if I don't kiss you on the mouth?" I said yes and got what I asked for.

We had one rule about sex. Position allowing, we look each other in the eye when we come. He describes his orgasm as five seconds in the hands of God, and I see that in his eyes when it happens. Watching him has gotten me off. Him watching me too. That night, everything about our sex was wrong. It was as if he didn't care how I felt. Like he wanted to get it over with. When he came (which he did quickly), his eyes were flat, soulless, and far from divine. I did not come that night.

Over toast and OJ, I got the morning speech from Alex: "I've decided to go away for a few weeks. This is not fear of intimacy or fear of commitment, so tell Santina to shut up when she throws that at you. I just can't do this anymore. I'm responsible for too many things in this relationship. More than I can handle. And this isn't because of last night. The pressure is too much. It's as if you can't accept anything less than total ecstasy at all times, and I'm sorry, Wanda, I don't have that in me. I hate it that I don't make you happy. And I hate you for not being happy with me. Don't say you are. It's not like you can hide your disappointment. And your transparency—you should do something about that.

"I don't like feeling so inadequate. I'm not blaming you, but I've never felt this way before with any of my old girlfriends. I thought I could deal with it—you know, stay with you and sleep in your bed until you figured it out. But I don't think I can wait for you to leave me anymore. So, I'm leaving before I say or do anything I regret."

I bit toast. "Why don't you say what you really mean?" I asked.

"That's exactly what I mean, Wanda. I can't even walk out the right way for you."

"You'll miss me."

"I'm sure I will."

"I won't take you back."

"My parents' anniversary is next week, so I'm going to Los Angeles to see them."

I said, "I should have let you sleep last night."

"It's not just last night."

"If you leave now, then it's completely over."

"I used one of your garbage bags for my stuff."

"You do make me happy."

"Your saying that just makes me want to run faster."

"But I love you."

"I don't think I love you." That's when a stampede of buffalo came barreling into my kitchen and trampled Alex into a fine pulp. No—actually, that's when I flung my glass of orange juice at him. I hit him in the chest. He didn't change before he left. My last memory is of that orange splotch on his white Gap T. Since then, the mere mention of the word *Tropicana* jabs me in the gut like a pin in a voodoo doll.

As fate would have it, Alex was wearing an orange T-shirt that night at the Outhouse. I'd be lying if I said his violent display didn't turn me on. I'd never seen him like that before. He left after what seemed like hours but was just a half-second, and I resumed breathing as best I could in my mini. Every droplet of blood in my body raced to my head. Seeing Alex sucked out loud. Hearing that he'd been Flush's boyfriend only made it suck harder. Crip Beluga was huddled against the bar. Crutch'd decided to play nursemaid and she crouched next to him, cooing in his ear. Then Crip started hollering.

"The pain, the pain. I can't stand the pain!" He was acting like a little kid who knows he's been hurt only when Mommy makes a fuss.

"Get out of the way," I said, pushing Crutch over. She fell back on nature's shock absorber and tried to spike me in the neck with her polished nails. "Try that again and you'll be eating your pancreas for dinner." She backed off. Crip moaned. His jaw was already beginning to swell. I placed my hands on either side of his face to see if it was broken. It wasn't. He'd hurt for a few days, but that was it. Even at the height of anger, Alex held himself back. He could have demolished Crip's jaw forever. "I hope you like soup, Crip baby."

"I'm going blind. I can't see."

"It's broken in about five hundred places." So I lied.

"The lights, they're going dim. Someone, hold my hand."

"The docs will probably want to wire your mouth shut for two, three years."

"Lordie, lordie, I'm too young to die."

He was delirious. What some people will do for attention. I stood up and said, "I'd better call the cops," which cleared the room faster than if I'd screamed fire. Crutch, loyal as a hounddog, leapt to take my place at Crip's side. She hummed taps. Some comfort.

I walked behind the bar to the fridge. An ice compress was all he really needed. I opened the freezer. Sandwiched between two ten-pound bags of ice was what looked like a red Louisville Slugger. I pried it out and saw it was just a frozen two-foot-long salami. Must have weighed twenty pounds. Why anyone would freeze a salami was beyond me. It stuck to my hands, so I grabbed a bar rag to hold it. On closer inspection, I saw dark brown freckles on the tip I took for dried blood, as well as a few black hairs clinging to the freeze. Finally I sighed. A clue.

"Eeek," shrieked Crutch when she saw it.

Crip, eyelids fluttering, said, "What in the dang-blazes is that?"

"It's what we hard-boiled types call a blunt object. Notice, if you will, the hairs—black like someone's we knew—stuck on the end here. Also, note what appear to be clumps of frozen brain matter."

"That must be what killed Flush!" triumphed Crip.

"Honey bear, you're so smart," gushed Crutch.

"Yes," I said, "for an idiot, he's a genius." My choices: take the murder weapon/blood message tool to Dick and Bucky, take it to Strom, or leave it where I found it. The killer might have left it there on purpose to be discovered. If no one did, he or she would go out of his or her way to make sure it was. If the killer hadn't had the opportunity to retrieve it, he or she would try sooner or later. So, I decided to leave it. That plan wouldn't work if Crip or Crutch talked, or if one of them was the killer. I remembered what Alex had said before he slammed Crip: "I know you did it." Blast, I thought. Now I'd have to see Alex again to find out what he meant. And that would be as pleasant as bone marrow extraction.

I replaced the deadly salami in the freezer and got my coat and bag in Crip's office. When I returned to the casino, Crutch was pouring Johnny Walker into

Crip. His nose and jaw were swollen like a blowfish. I said, "I'm off. If the killer finds out we found the murder weapon, we might end up dead. I want you both to promise you won't tell anyone about it."

They nodded. I knew they'd blab within the hour. I fondled Mama in my bag to relax me. I decided to have a talk with Strom. I was being jerked in too many directions, and my patience was up.

Crip said, "You can tell that Alex Beaudine friend of yours that Crip Beluga doesn't sleep. I'll find him, and when I do, I'll stuff him up like a two-headed calf." Not if I get to him first, I thought. I'd save that for later. My stomach growled. I hadn't eaten dinner. I dug around in my pockets.

"I need money." I'd left my wad at home. Crip pshawed and told Crutch to give me her tips.

She scowled and said, "You're a cheap bastard, honey bear. But I love you anyway." She went into Crip's office and came back with a folded twenty. She winked when she forked it over, which I thought strange. I put the bill in my pocket and split.

After midnight in the East Village is like free-play at the asylum. Bars overflow with every kind of trendoid —among them Earth children, retro-punks, slumming yuppies, tortured artists, and pseudo-intellectuals. The style is intensity. The fashion: at least one article of black clothing per dweller. The mood is expectant. What I've always loved about strolling through the nabe, more than any other in New York, is the feeling that anything could happen— be it a ricochet bullet to the head or love at first sight. Neither happened to me that Wednesday night. In search of pizza, I slogged by the Gaze Craze crystal shop, the Aroma Arena incense shop, several bondage-wear emporiums, and at least four Italian delis with strands of blood sausage links dangling in the windows. Locating the killer salami maker wouldn't be easy.

Tenth Street is the marijuana capital of the world. As I stood at the corner, waiting for the light to change, a customer in a Mets cap approached one of the Colombian sellers posted at his stoop. Mets said, "Got any skunk?" The dealer said yes, (which he inevitably would, even if all he had was oregano). The buyer asked for two and handed over a twenty. The dealer opened his garbage can and untaped two dime bags adhering to the lid. Mets took a whiff to make sure it was skunk, nodded, and walked away toward Second Avenue. The whole transaction took ten seconds, max. Otherwise, business was slow. It was snowing. I didn't know for how long—the drapes at the Outhouse obscured any view of the street. My feet were drenched, heels being inadequate snow-protection. I should have worn my galoshes.

I didn't see the limo right away. A homeless person on a subway grate whispered, "Coming up the rear, baby," and I turned to look. Inching toward me, the six-door limo had thick, black bulletproof windows. The paint job was sharkskin gray. I tried to make out the driver, but I couldn't see much through the snow or the windows. The limo stopped and double-parked right by the pot-dealer's stoop. I turned and stared at the street light. A motorcycle roared by on the avenue. I heard the echo of laughter coming out of a bar at the corner. A car backfired somewhere close. Curiosity forced me to turn back to the limo. As I scanned around, I noticed that the homeless person and the dealer had disappeared. The limo remained. But even though it was just feet away, I couldn't see it. All I could see was the five-inch barrel of a Colt .45 pointed straight at my nose.

Instinctively, I reached for Mama in my purse. The three-hundred pound goon attached to the gun stopped me. He had hands like dinner plates. "Move that arm and lose it, sister," he advised. I wondered how much damage he'd do if I teased him about his male-pattern baldness. He looked me over and said, "Bismark is so damned predictable."

"North Dakota?" I asked.

"Herring, baby. Get in the car." He dug the barrel into my chin.

I got in the car. The back compartment of the limo was as big as the Do It Right office, but warmer. There was a wet bar, a little fridge, and a color TV flashing the late show. A Bette Davis movie. The name escaped me. A tiny white-bearded man was watching the flick, cozy in silk pajamas and drinking a diet Coke. The goon slid in next to me. He kept the gun aimed at my chest. We waited for a commercial.

Finally, the old man said softly, "Gigantor, you know I hate guns." The goon leaned way back to fit the heater under his belt. The old man faced me. "I'm Nicolaus Vespucci. I've got a lot of nicknames, but the one most used is Saint Nick. I'm a private investor. And you are a private detective. That must be very interesting. I'd love you to tell me all about it some day." He held out his spotty little hand to shake. I shook.

"Wanda Mallory. No nicknames."

"Everyone should have a nickname. I'll call you, hmm. Just give me a second. I'm very good at this. I name everyone I know. Yes, I see you as, well . . . Hmm. This is odd. Nothing comes to mind."

"I think this is why I never had one."

"We can get back to that. I'm starving. You?"

Yes, dying. I said, "No, thanks." Nick reached into the fridge and pulled out a roll of pepperoni. He cut into the meat the long way and began gnawing and tearing off huge chunks at a time. I'd never seen anyone devour pepperoni with such abandon. The garlic rush was heavenly.

"Are you sure you don't want any?" he asked. "You look like you do."

So my mouth waters. "No, really. I'm fine."

"I guess you're wondering why I had Gigantor abduct you like that."

"I wouldn't have minded a simple invitation."

"Violence is such a bother, I know. I'm sorry about that, but this society demands it. If I could do things the way I'd like, I'd have sent you a proper request. Gigantor's gun was just insurance—to make sure you'd come see me." His eyebrows tilted up in the middle. It made him look like a kindly old crossing guard.

"I'm here, so what's the beef?" He paused for a nosh. As he bit down, I caught a glimpse of his teeth. They were spiked and sharp.

He spoke slowly and gently. "Wanda, we need to talk, about a mutual friend of ours. It's very important to his security and yours that you do not lie to me. I realize that lying, like violence, is unavoidable in modern times. So I'd understand your temptation to lie, just like you understand my temptation to use weaponry. If you do lie to me, I'm going to have Gigantor break your fingers. All right?"

"Sounds reasonable." But his plan didn't make sense. How would he know I was lying? I said, "Before you start asking me questions, you have to answer a few first. I think that's fair."

"Hmm. Well, no, I don't think so. Sorry, Wanda. I'm sure you understand." His condescension was clear, and his speech started to sound like he was talking to a foreigner, child, or someone missing a few chromosomes. I decided to fuck with him.

"Fire when ready," I prompted.

"Strom Bismark hired you to locate some missing money, correct?"

"No."

"You said no?"

"Strom hired me to protect his money."

"You're saying Strom hasn't lost any money."

"Yes." Nick paused. He smiled, and his teeth reminded me of dinosaurs.

"And Flush Royale. The police don't seem to have any idea what's going on there."

"Neither do I."

"And has anyone found a murder weapon?"

"No."

"Any suspects?"

"You'll have to ask the cops."

"Do you think she died painfully?" His eyebrows tilted again. I could tell he wanted the answer to be no.

"She didn't feel a thing."

"To sum up, Strom hired you to protect money which has not been misplaced or removed. To your knowledge, no murder weapon had been found and that Flush died painlessly."

"Roger."

"I'd like you to relay a message from me to Strom. Please tell him that he's done himself quite a service to hire an obviously capable, smart and, if you don't mind an old man's opinion, very attractive young woman. Also, tell him he's got a week or we ride out to Queens. Also, tell him to eat more vegetables."

"Queens and vegetables. You got it."

"You may go." We shook hands goodbye. I wondered why Strom was so afraid of this man. So he had a bodyguard. Lars was younger and could easily flatten Gigantor. Besides that, I'd lied three times, and I was walking out with all my fingers in their sockets. I smiled smugly to myself. I'm so smooth. I'm so cool. I was born to sleuth.

Gigantor moved to the other side of the limo compartment so I could get out. I pulled the door handle, but it didn't budge—locked. I turned to Nick, but he was ignoring me, once again absorbed by the late show.

"Hey, Gigantor, spring me," I said.

"You didn't shake." I took that to mean I hadn't formally bid farewell to the balding giant. I held out my hand. Instead of offering his own, Gigantor grabbed me by the wrist. With his other dinner dish, he used a motion too quick to study (in the nanosecond, it looked like a pinch) and snapped my pinky above the knuckle, adding an exclamation pop to Bette Davis in a black dress. I actually saw stars. The pain was immediate and fierce and sadistically local. Years ago, when I broke my arm by falling off a horse named Ted, I felt dull throbs all over my body. This time, the stabbing concentrated on the exact spot. I cried out and felt guilty for having given Crip a hard time earlier. Physical agony is not funny.

Gigantor threw back his head and laughed expansively. He flipped a switch and the door unlocked. He opened it and booted me out onto the street, into the snow.

"You filthy barbarian," I yelled as he got in the driver's seat. "My finger will heal. But in five years, you won't have any hair!" But they were already slush in the wind. The gray shark sailed down First Avenue, and I stood up in my heels. The fishnets were ruined, and I'd never wear a pinky ring again. A free cab pulled up out of nowhere. I found that to be very yin-yang. I flung myself against the back seat and sprawled out. My finger throbbed. I pleaded, "Ludlow and Delancey."

The cabbie said, "You must show me."

I groaned, struggled upright, and showed Ashana Shamirez the way. It cost only three-fifty, so I paid him with the coin reserves on the bottom of my bag. I stumbled to Alex's door in the vise grip of blinding agony. Well, maybe not that bad. I held a finger over his buzzer, but hesitated. I did the analytical girl thing and wondered if I was running to Alex so that he would take pity on me and allow me back into his life. Was I cowardly, running to him when I could take care of myself? I wondered if he'd let me spend the night. In his bed, perhaps. I wondered if that was such a good idea. I lowered my hand and took a deep breath. My pinky had gone numb from thwarted circulation and the cold. It still hurt like a motherfucker—I'm not that brave. I walked up Ludlow Street. I patted myself on the back for being so grown up.

I got as far as East Houston before I ran back.

CHAPTER FOUR

Out of the Frying Pan and Into the Nuclear Reactor

F*zzz.* "Hello?" said Alex through the intercom.

"It's Wanda. Buzz me in."

I waited. Nothing. I leaned harder on the button.

Fzzz. "I can't deal with you right now."

"What the hell do you mean by that? Are you saying I'm difficult? Look, buster, you aren't the one freezing your ass off on the street with your pinky snapped in half."

Fzzz. "I've got problems of my own."

"Alex, goddam it." My throat caught. "I need you."

Click. The lock sprung. Alex's apartment is on the sixth floor of a walk-up (the exercise floor, he says). I wasn't that out of breath when I finished the hike. The door was ajar. I went in. His studio, one room with a closet-sized kitchen, seemed even punier than I remembered. The toilet was still in the shower. Every inch of vertical space was decorated with framed photographs and the book shelves he had built himself. He rearranged the books constantly. The pictures were colorful and not all his. Have I mentioned that Alex is a photographer? Formerly for fashion magazines, later for Do It Right. He also collected antique furniture from Salvation Army stores—bright Fifties Deco stuff—which crammed all the available floor space. He had particular affection for a black lacquered table with a blue glass top that he unearthed at a rummage sale on the Jersey shore. No one was allowed to put their feet or a coasterless glass on it. The throw rug was a purple Indian weave. Strands of film negatives hung from roach clips on a piece of chicken wire tacked to the ceiling. Which was low, maybe eight feet. (Alex, in his six-foot glory, could touch it, standing on his toes.) Compared to my spacious digs, Alex's place was downright claustrophobic. And annoyingly neat. He was a compulsive straightener.

"Up here," he said from atop his loft bed. It was about five feet off the floor. No ladder. The first night I spent there, he told me the story of one former girlfriend who couldn't make the vault. She was so embarrassed, she never came back.

I circled the room. I glanced at him in his boxers on the bed. You'd think he'd have the decency to put clothes on. "What's different?" I asked. There had been a change, but I couldn't tell what. I sat down in a cushy green module chair, careful not to jostle my busted finger.

"You mean the floor," he said. That was it. The black-and-white square tiles were gone. "I ripped up the tiles a few months ago. Bored, I guess. The wood needs staining. I haven't had time to get around to it yet."

"A few months ago. You mean around the time we broke up."

"Around then," replied Alex.

"I thought you were in California."

"I never quite made it out."

"So you tore your floor apart instead."

"Not that day."

"But that week."

"Does it matter?"

"What other hostile, violent acts of transference did you commit? Is this the new you? A vicious brute whose only pleasure is destruction?"

"Here we go," he sighed.

"Was it guilt, Alex?"

"Jesus."

"Or was it anger? Or maybe you couldn't spend any more time kicking yourself for losing me."

"I just wanted to change the floor."

"Alex, you idiot. Nothing in life is just wanting to change anything."

"Thanks for clearing that up."

"I mean nothing's so simple."

"What happened to your hair? Run over by a tar truck?"

"I wanted a change."

"I thought nothing was so simple."

"Shut up, Alex. You know zero about me." The reunion progressed swimmingly. I guess it's fair to say I was hard on him. My finger ached. The vise grip of paralyzing agony was back, in my head too. Alex jumped down from the loft and came over to me.

"Let me see," he said, cradling my hand. "I have some Frozfruit in the freezer. Be right back." He padded to his kitchen. I noticed no dirt stuck to his feet. He ran hot water in the dirty-dishless sink and melted the pops down to sticks. I was glad for the chance to ogle him, even though I knew it would dredge up too many happy memories. There's a lot to be said for sleeping with gorgeous men. Just watching is a treat. I don't think I'll be able to go back. He finished quickly and returned.

Alex kneeled in front of me and yanked my pinky as upright as it would go. The contact with him didn't balance out the pain. He wrapped the sticks on with dental floss. "This should do for now," he said. "But get Shlomo to do a real job for you later." Shlomo Zambini is Santina's fiancé. He's also an orthopedic surgeon. For some reason, it upset me that Alex knew about other people in my life.

"What happened?" he asked.

"You look beautiful." A terrible move, saying something heartfelt and honest.

"So do you."

"You like the hair?"

"I hate it, but you look great. Have you lost weight?"

"Are you saying I was fat before?"

"Of course not."

"So why'd you live with me if you thought I was fat?"

"Do you think we can have a conversation that doesn't end at five-hundred decibels?"

"I'm not here for pleasant conversation."

"Then, why are you here?"

Good question. I think it had something to do with the shape of his long, uncovered legs. "I'm here on business. I'm working for Strom Bismark. I need information on Flush Royale. That's why I was at the Outhouse tonight."

"You're joking. Strom Bismark could eat you alive."

"I'm absolutely serious. And if anyone's being eaten alive, it's Strom."

71

"What do you mean by that?"

"A woman has her wiles."

"So now I'm to assume you're sleeping with him. And I'm supposed to get all jealous and beg you to come back to me."

"Begging wouldn't do it, Alex." But it'd be a start.

"So you won't be disappointed when I don't."

"Fuck this," I said. "I'm leaving."

"You know where the door is." I stood up. He sat Indian-style on the floor, the hole in his boxers opened slightly. I couldn't see anything good—I should have worn my glasses. I thought about a game we used to play in bed together. I would tell Alex fairy tales while he tried to distract me to the point where I couldn't talk anymore. We also gave each other full body rubs with jasmine-scented massage oil. I didn't cry when we split. That would have made it worse.

I walked slowly to the door, one careful step after the other. The studio was so small, I made quick progress. I had my hand on the knob when he stopped me.

"I guess this is why we broke up," he said sadly.

"The fighting?"

"No. I sort of like the fighting. I don't know."

"Do you think it's the job?" I've thought that before. I spend so much energy cleaning up other people's lives, I make a mess of my own.

"I don't know. I am sure of one thing, Wanda—"

I waited.

He continued, "If we got back together we'd probably kill each other."

"What, as in die of happiness?"

He sighed. "I don't want a life that you're not a part of. I didn't leave because I didn't love you."

"You're talking in negatives."

"I can't say how I feel. If I say anything, I'll be committed to it."

The thought of a life without him didn't seem too rosy for me either. A light bulb blinked. "Let's work together," I said. "Like we did before. For Do It Right. No part of my body will touch any part of your body."

"You think that's possible?"

"Just for this case. We'll see how it goes. Besides, you're involved whether you want to be or not."

"You mean Flush."

"Your girlfriend." The words tasted lousy in my mouth.

"We weren't sleeping together. She was helping me."

"I bet."

"I'm doing a photo documentary on Blood & Iron. I talked to a book editor in midtown. She wants it, and Flush was my way in. I only met her two months ago, when I was hanging around the Outhouse. We were just friends."

A likely story, one that doesn't explain his eruptive reaction to the news of her demise. And how dare he get on with his life so soon after we broke up? I pointed to the negatives hanging from the wire. "These B&I shots?"

"Most." He lazily readjusted his boxers. "Wanda, I don't know if this is a good idea. Just being in the same room with you makes me feel funny."

"Like you want to kiss me?" I used my sexy voice, which can sound like I have a cold.

"More than that." I smiled. He looked worried. "I think you'd better go," he said. "I'll meet you at Do It Right at the crack of dawn: 10:00 A.M. I'll make some prints and tell you everything I know."

"I won't wear something special." An "in" joke—I

73

used to say that to him when I went without underwear. He blushed. I surprised myself by leaving without a fight.

Delancey Street was deserted. It was after two. The
snow had stopped. He'd more or less admitted that he
still wanted me. Knowing that was as good as the real
thing. (Who am I kidding?) I cabbed home to Brooklyn and woke up a disgruntled Shlomo to take care of
my finger. He gave me a Valium. I made a mental note
before I had the first deep sleep all month: waiting
isn't always the hardest part.

Otis woke me with her morning air sortie from my
dresser onto my stomach. It was 9:00 A.M. I pushed
her aside, groggy from drugged slumber, but she
pounced back and milked my gut with her paws. She
crept forward and suckled my ears. It tickled. I
hugged her too hard and she jumped off, trotting from
my bedroom toward the kitchen. I groped for a
cigarette on my nightstand and fired it up, my first of
many that day. It tasted swell. I stared at the ceiling.
There was a web in one corner, with spider. My finger
throbbed. I groaned and fell out of bed.

I'd paid for the cab home with the money Crutch
gave me. The driver mumbled something when he
handed me the change, I didn't remember what. After
I fed Otis breakfast—Prime Grill—I checked the
fridge for myself. Nothing. No surprise. It'd been a
while since I saw any human food. I threw on sweats
and my Donna Karan and ran to the deli across the
street for a bagel. It was a coffee morning. Even
though java wreaks hell on my delicate innards, I
needed the jolt. The counterman poured the injection
and I dug in my pockets for bucks. When I pulled out

my cab change, I saw it. The yellow post-it note with a message to me stuck to the bill.

Once home and munching, I gave it a careful inspection. The script was slanting to the right. That means the writer is always looking ahead. (I learned about that in my *Autographology of the Stars*. I'm an impulse shopper.) Crutch must have stuck the Post-It to the twenty-spot before she forked it over the night before. Thank God the cabbie noticed it and gave it back. It said: "Ask Strom about his tattoo. Then ask me. I'm older than I look, and smarter than you think. My real name is Sally." She must have meant the dagger on his left hand. I'd figured it was a B&I thing. I must have been wrong. I wondered what Alex knew about Crutch. I showered with difficulty, unable to use one hand. I put on a Gordon Henderson oversized sweater and leggings. I was running late—it was already quarter to ten. I cut a hole in a mitten for my bad hand, grabbed the collection of newspaper clips on the gang, and ran to Seventh and Flatbush for the subway.

I prepared my speech for Alex on the D train to Times Square. ETA: 35 minutes. "Alex, when you left, you ripped the heart from my chest, flung it to the ground, stomped on it, and let tiny black insects devour it, throw it up, and eat it again. I'm not blaming you. Please, don't feel guilty. I'm fine now. Really." That might have been a bit much. I didn't want to terrorize him.

"Life is to be explored," I'd postulate. "It's being lost in the jungle on a starless night, snarls and growls all around. To proceed with caution wouldn't make a difference. I've never gotten back together with a lover before . . . and I don't think you have, either. Let's try it. Expand our realms of experience. Forge ahead in the jungle. If it works, beautiful. If not, we'll be torn to shreds. All you have to do, honey, is lay one on me."

He'd say, "We've done that. We know what it's like."

"Not since the breakup. It's new ground. Virgin earth to unturn and conquer."

"A kiss won't make a difference."

"One kiss could change our lives." Wretched, I know, but Alex liked a healthy dose of sentimentalism. He'd kiss me, we'd collapse to the floor and ravage each other in a fit of volcanic passion. He'd move back to my place, and in no time, I'd have him hooked. Under control.

As usual, my plan failed miserably. I was twenty minutes late to Do It Right. My mouth was dry and my lips were chapped from the jog across 42nd Street. Alex was waiting, obviously annoyed. "You're late," he said. "I made prints."

He wore 501s, white Converse high-tops and a Gap T. His hair was flopped over one eye. He pushed it back and his lucid brown pearls hit me in stereo. It sent my heart aflutter. I blurted, "I love you and I want you back." So I have trouble with subtlety.

"And I thought Flush was hit over the head."

"Ignore that," I said in a fluster. "I have no idea where that came from. Look, just give me the prints and shut up."

Alex twisted the corners of his mouth into an adorable smile. It was more for my embarrassment than for my offer. I sifted through the pile for something to do. The pictures were a new direction for Alex. He used to take portraits and close-ups only. I never told him, but I always thought they were flat. These were group shots of strangers. Dangerous faces and bodies in motion. The quality was raw and angry. Frenzied. They were sensational.

"Alex, these are good." I felt proud of him.

"You think so?"

"How much money will you get for this book?"

"She won't talk money until I get an agent."

"You don't have one?"

"I'm working on it." He was getting edgy.

"None of these pictures are inside B&I headquarters."

"I haven't made it in yet. I have to get clearance from Smith Jones."

"Smith Jones?"

"Number Two. He's Strom's enforcer."

"Not Lars?"

"Lars is Strom's personal enforcer. Smith handles the gang."

Alex found a picture of him in the pile. Smith, in front of the B&I building, was with three other men, all much larger and stupider. He was sinewy and tight as a wound spring in overalls, a leather jacket, and cowboy boots with spurs. He had long, blond hair in a ponytail, and his mouth was opened like he was screaming. Alex said, "I don't know these other guys by name. They're just soldiers."

"And what do they do?"

He said, "What do you think?" I shrugged. "They bloody people and steal cars."

"I knew that." I flipped to another picture. "Could a soldier have killed Flush? On command?"

"Crip Beluga did it."

"No chance. He's too vain to kill."

"Therein lies the proof—his unrequited lust gone awry."

"Do elaborate, Watson."

"Flush'd been at the Outhouse for a month when I met her. Crip had been coming on like a linebacker. She'd have nothing to do with him, but the more she told him to leave her alone, the more he wanted her. She told me he was beginning to scare her, so I told Crip to lay off. That's why he thinks we were sleeping together. She played it up, and I think she convinced herself she had a crush on me."

"I'm sure you did nothing to encourage her. She was a real bowser."

He rolled over it. "Crip left her alone for a few days. But the first night I didn't show, he cornered Flush in his office. I think an older woman could have gotten herself out of it more gracefully. But Flush was young and excitable. He grabbed her and she cut him across the cheek with a nail file. He threatened to kill her, but she escaped. She came over and told me what happened. That was the last time I saw her." And Crip told me his mother gave him that scar. I suppose he's got a bridge to sell me too.

I said, "A week later Flush winds up dead in Crip's office? It's bunk, Alex. Way too easy." I was surprised he didn't know that.

"You should have heard him at the club the next day."

"Lots of dang-blasts and hog-ties?"

"He lost the accent."

"That pissed, huh?" I lit a cigarette and pondered. "On pure vibe levels, I don't buy it. From what I've seen of Crip, he doesn't have the nuts." Alex smirked at my dismissal. A theory is one thing, but Crip's guilt seemed too important to him. "I'm curious about something," I said. "You're a hamster. Hamsters don't hit people."

"They do when they're provoked. Especially boy hamsters."

"From whence provocation?"

"He killed Flush. That's not enough for you?"

"Hmm." I inhaled smoke. "What do you know about Crutch?"

"Not much," he said. "She just started working there a week ago, when Flush left. I'd only seen her one time before last night."

"She's balling Crip." I waited for a reaction. Nothing. I told Alex quickly about finding the salami and Crutch's note. And then about my run-in with Nick Vespucci and Gigantor. Alex tensed visibly.

"Don't hold out on me," I warned.

"This Nick, what does he look like?"

"He's old, seventy maybe. Skinny. White beard. Mildly osteoporotic."

"Did you notice his teeth?"

"Shark, vicious, could puncture a jugular."

"That's him. I was at Flush's apartment one night when he showed up with the big guy. She kicked me out when they got there. She made me promise not to mention seeing him to anyone. She was doing a job for him. I got the feeling it was dangerous, because she wouldn't talk about it again."

"What were you doing in her apartment?" I asked.

"Just talking." I squashed out my cigarette. Just talking, my ass. Alex, the mature one, had a thing for younger women. He'd never admit it, but I'd seen his eyes chase high school girls up and down the block. I suddenly tasted my twenty-eight years, and they weren't sweet. Alex was twenty-seven. His birthday was in August. He must have slept with her at least once. I could smell it.

The phone rang. "Mallory," I barked into the receiver.

"Bismark," said the voice on line.

"Hi, Strom." I looked at Alex. He locked his eyes on me like a cat's on goldfish. I used my sexy voice. "I met your friend Nick Vespucci last night. He gave me a message for you."

"Do you have a cold?" he asked.

"No. Look, Strom, we need to talk."

"Tonight. Come to the headquarters."

"What time?" I asked. Alex found a scrap of paper on my desk. He scribbled and showed me. It said I should tell Strom he was on the job. I shook my head and gestured for him to keep quiet.

"Get here by six. I'll cook dinner," said Strom.

"What a good wife you'll make."

"What do you mean?" he asked.

"Later," I said and hung up.

Alex was angry. He said, "I thought we were partners."

"I know what I'm doing, Alex. This is my show."

"This is Strom's show," he said ominously.

It was my show as long as I was getting paid, but I didn't share that with Alex. He'd give me a speech about right and wrong. I try not to think about that. I have an inherent moral instinct—whatever I can stomach is right. What makes me vomit is wrong. I was sure I could stomach dinner with Strom.

I pulled out my mound of newspaper clippings on Strom and Blood & Iron from the plastic deli bag. I gave half to Alex and told him to look for money stories. He sat down in the lumpy Ethan Allen client chair. He started reading. I did the same.

I tried to concentrate, but something Crip said kept jabbing its way into my consciousness. It seemed like a passable time to bring it up. "So you're saying Crip's a loon?" I asked. Alex looked up and nodded. "When I was questioning him about Flush, he said I was responsible for her murder."

"Why would he say that?"

"I figured you might have some idea."

"How would I know?"

"Crip said he knew who I really was."

"I still don't see what that has to do with me."

"Maybe you said something to Flush about your past as a private dick and my name came up."

"That was three months ago. My past is when I lost my virginity."

"Another revealing connection."

"I'm only involved because I'm working for Do It Right." He forced a smile. I responded with a blank glare. He said, "Crip and I don't get along. He'd say anything to get to me. Even through you."

"And all you did was protect Flush?" He nodded. I didn't believe him—partly because of my suspicious nature, partly out of jealousy. I tried to keep professional. Instead, I said, "Swear to me you never slept with her."

He pushed some hair off his face and crossed his arms over his thin chest. He stared over my shoulder when he said, "I swear."

The lie was so obvious, I almost spit. He was never very good at deception. Maybe he lied to spare my feelings, maybe because he was up to his short hairs in this mess and didn't want me to know it. Whatever. The cause wasn't so important. The effect was devastating. First my client, and now I couldn't trust my partner either. Even flanked by men, I rode solo.

* * *

I was twenty minutes late to B&I headquarters. Large Lars, doubling as maitre d' and head waiter, rushed me into Strom's library. A romantic dinner for two had been arranged—candles, crystal, red wine, and porcelain flatware. The works. Strom had yet to make his entrance. I'd assumed I was the only guest, but those leather-bound toes poking out from under the drapes must have been invited too. I pretended I didn't notice them. There was a scratch sound, and then Sinatra singing "Night and Day" flowed out through hidden speakers. I'd expected something more metallic. Lars took my coat and pulled out a chair for me, my back to the curtained wall. Then he left me alone with the shoes. I took Mama out of my bag, fondled it for luck, and dropped her in my lap. I unfolded my napkin and hid her with it.

Strom appeared under the Satanic arch. He was decked out—tuxedo jacket, black shirt with a black tie, faded jeans, work boots, and a wicked smile. And messy me, in my Gordon sweater and Doc Martens. I wished I'd changed. He took a seat and poured the wine. He noticed my bandaged pinky. "How'd that happen?" he asked.

"Slipped on the snow." He licked his lips suggestively. I said, "Why do I get the feeling this isn't a business dinner."

"We can talk business."

"Then you can write it off."

"That's what I love about you, Wanda. You're full of good ideas." I wondered if that included my handcuff fantasy.

He raised his glass. "Here's to our first case together." I waited for him to sip. He didn't fall down, so I drank too.

"You're a lefty," I said while admiring his tattoo. So was Alex.

"I'm a lefty but I do everything right."

"I'll take your word for it."

"After tonight, you won't have to." I must have looked surprised, because he laughed. "Don't be scared, Wanda. I won't bite."

"I sort of hoped you would." He looked surprised that time. Tie score.

Strom clapped his hands twice. A mean, hairy biker trotted in with a silver tray. He wore an apron but looked like he could gnaw through granite. Strom motioned to the table, and the hulk deposited the tray. He trotted out. Strom lifted the cover to display roast duck with sauce á l'orange, couscous with raisins, and what appeared to be stuffed zucchini boats. How could he know? It was my favorite meal. He served me and then himself. The first bite was luscious. The second, divine squared. I wondered why people didn't say the way to a girl's heart is through her stomach. We ate in silence for a while, my pleasure heightened by the weight of Mama in my lap.

Finally, Strom asked, "Saint Nick gave you a message for me?"

"This is incredible. I can't believe you made it yourself."

"It pleases me that you enjoyed it."

"He said you've got a week, or you ride to Queens."

"Anything else?"

"Eat more veggies."

"Cocksucker."

"How do you know?"

"Not you. He has me over a barrel, Wanda. I need that money fast."

83

"What's so horrible in Queens?"

"Rikers Island," he said and ate a forkful of duck. "This *is* good. I outdid myself tonight."

"So, he's got something on you?" I asked.

"In a complicated way, yes. But you don't need to know about that."

I tilted my glass at his hand. "Something to do with that tattoo, perhaps?" He froze mid-fork-lift. "Let me tell you how I earned my fee today. I sat in my office for six hours, reading every newspaper piece from the past ten years on you and your gang. I know more about you than your proctologist. One particularly interesting mention on Page Seven captured my attention. About Bisque-Mark, Inc.? Surely you remember it." I took a triumphant sip of wine.

He didn't flinch. "A former journalist like yourself should know not to believe everything you read." Touché. So he knows about me too. I had been a fact-checker/reporter for a porn-for-ladies rag called *Midnight*. That was years ago. My boss got strangled to death after I quit. Alex and I solved her murder, but that's another story.

"Here's what I do believe," I started. "With Nick's loan, you created a corporation to produce and distribute the Bisque-Mark Blade, the first-of-its-kind ceramic stiletto. That tattoo looks a whole lot like the logo. The company went belly-up almost immediately when the blades started puckering in potters' kilns. Didn't it occur to you to make a model first? You can't do much damage stabbing someone with a clay pickle."

The tornado behind his green eyes churned. "Are you calling me stupid?" he asked.

"Not me, Strom. But the *Wall Street Journal* did."

He fought for control of his facial muscles, and I hoped he'd crack. His inhuman control unsettled me. My hand instinctively brushed over my heater. I was ready for the tempest, but it never came. He gently patted his mouth with his napkin and clapped twice. The apron-clad biker trotted in, removed the dishes, and disappeared. Strom pulled two cigarettes out of his case and lit both. He handed one to me. "Why ask for the moon?" I quipped.

"They're Marlboros," he said. I'd played my trump card, and Strom barely blinked. The frustration made me reckless. That, and the tightening of his lips around the cigarette.

I had one trick left and decided to play it hard and fast. At that point, I would have done anything to see him jump. Pretending to yawn, I stealthily tucked Mama into the back of my leggings. I stood up and stretched. With calculated randomness, I patrolled the library. Strom watched me from the table. I checked my look in the huge framed mirror, running my fingers through my raven hair. In the reflection, I registered the toes poking out from under the drapes. I walked backward from the mirror, my image shrinking with each step. When close enough, I spun and grabbed Mama in one motion. I pointed the little four-inch barrel at the drapes where I thought the interloper's head would be. I cocked the trigger and turned to Strom. "What do we have here, Strom? One of your minions?" Strom took a sip of wine. "Should I shoot first and ask questions later?"

Strom said, "By all means, Wanda, shoot."

I inched toward the wall. "I'll do it, Strom," I warned.

"Let's see how tough you are."

I re-aimed elaborately, squinting with one eye. "You've got five seconds to come out, or I start shooting."

Strom laughed. He said, "Why wait?"

I started counting down. "Five, four . . ."

"He won't come out unless I say."

"Three, two . . ."

"He'd die for me, Wanda."

"One and a half, one and a quarter . . ."

"I guess I was right about you."

"I don't care if you breastfed him, Strom. No one's loyalty is fierce enough to die for."

"The price of betrayal is higher."

I pointed my gun at the ceiling and squeezed the trigger. The explosion echoed in the cavernous room. Pieces of crystal chandelier tinkled onto the Oriental rug. A few bikers ran in from the sound of the blast. I fumbled with the drapes. They were heavy, and once I scooped them up, the interloper had already disappeared through the hidden door. I tried, but it was locked. Damn, I thought. I knew my dramatic flourish would fuck me up one of these days.

Strom waved the bikers out and sidled over to me. He put his arms around my shoulders and said, "You're shaking."

"Get away from me." He acted hurt—the first sign of any emotions at all from Strom. "You wanted me to kill him."

"No, I wanted him to run out screaming. I didn't even know he was there until you had your gun out."

"And the word *gullible*'s not in the dictionary."

"Sure it is." He didn't get it.

"I fucking quit," I said. "I'd rather puke blood from bad tequila than work for a monster like you. I'll keep your advance." I pushed past him and grabbed my

Donna Karan. He came up behind me and spun me around to face him. Something had changed in his green eyes. He looked sad and helpless, like the notion of me leaving would crush him. A huge threat to my resistance—I am a sucker for sad, helpless men. He put his hand on the back of my neck and his tongue in my mouth. He lifted me off the ground and pressed my body against his. I didn't know if I should scream for help or swoon with passion. He lowered me to my feet and I stumbled back, breathless. He'd sucked the fight (and the wind) out of me.

He said, "I'm sorry. I shouldn't have done that."

"Am I working for you, or not?" I asked.

"Stay tonight."

"This is my show, damnit."

He whispered the words, *Trust me, Wanda,* before he kissed me again. That time, I didn't struggle at all.

As he led me to the elevator down the hall, I'd felt stupider than I have in ages. I could hightail at any time—or I assumed I could—but the invisible fingers of lust prodded me along. Like an alcoholic to alcohol, I was powerless against them, plus, the element of fear never fails to excite me. We took the black-walled elevator to the third floor. Strom kept one hand under my sweater, on my spine. The doors creaked opened, and he steered me down the hall to the corner room.

Inside, it was dark as a space vacuum. I was led, groping in the blackness, to the bed. I sat on the edge and he said, "Strip from the waist down, lie on your back and spread your legs." I could make out only his outline.

I said, "I don't like sex in the dark."

He ignored me and kicked the door shut. The slam rocked the bed.

CHAPTER FIVE

Where's a Warm Puppy When You Need One?

I lit a cigarette. The glow from the lighter played on Strom's body, sleeping next to me. I inhaled and exhaled smoke like oxygen. My lips tasted salty. For a while, I considered the possibility of being his sex slave for all eternity. (Yes, he was that good.) It was an hour and half a pack of cigarettes before I shook off the bombardment of post-coital love waves and got up to go. I wondered if I should leave a card, a nice note, something to remind him I'd been there. I decided against it. He'd remember our night together. I knew I would, and I'd reflect back with pleasant memories, albeit soggy ones.

He stirred and the sheets fell off the bed. All men look like children when they sleep. I picked up the sheets and covered him, hating myself for being so maternal. I searched in the dark for my clothes. I stepped on something on the floor and it cracked. A lamp came on. I faced Strom. He was rubbing his eyes with his paws and scrunching his nose. I got a better view of the room with the lights on. It was sparse and warm, like my place, and messy over clean, unlike my place, which was messy over messy. I turned my attention to a naked Strom. Caramba, I thought. A crushed CD box was under my feet.

"I only broke one thing," I said.

He blinked, focused on me, and said, "Come back in bed."

"You must have made a pact with the Devil," I suggested. "Maybe you are the Devil." He sure fucked like him.

"Don't get dressed." He rolled onto his back, his hard-on calling like a beacon.

"I can't stay," I said. The mornings were cruel, and unless drunk or zonked, I preferred to split before them. Except with Alex, of course. Rules changed in love. I was not in love with Strom—lust, definitely. I picked up my sweater. He was a maniac in the sack, and, truth be told, I was afraid of what he might do to me.

"We need to talk," he said.

I went over and sat on the edge of the bed, expecting the standard "I'll call you" speech. But Strom pulled me to him and kissed me more gently than he had all night. He seemed like a different person with the lights on.

"I want you to know me, Wanda," he said. "Not many people understand why I do what I do. They try to figure me out, but in the end, they just do what I say."

He nudged my breast with his nose. The sweetness of him was killing me, and I found myself wanting desperately to help him. I said, "I feel the same way." But I didn't.

"The last person who really understood me was my mother," he confessed. I was stunned—nothing else about him was as typical. "Mom had some kind of stroke when I was little. My father tried to explain it to me, but I was too young to understand what happened. She got slow—like she was stuck in second gear. She got forgetful too. She left things burning on the stove, or she'd buy something and leave it at the store. Dad was convinced she'd hurt herself, and he told me to look out for her when he was working. So, I spent every second with her. I felt like we knew each other's thoughts. My father took off when I was six and a half. Couldn't take the change in her anymore. He told me that I'd be the man of the house from then on. I said *fuck* and *shit* a lot. Like Dad did. And I started to push Mom around too. She thought it was pretty cute, until I got big enough to hurt her. I don't know where Dad is now."

I stroked Strom's cheek. I reminded myself that information offered so voluntarily is suspect. "Did your mother remarry?" I asked.

"Didn't get the chance. I was playing with matches in her closet and a dress caught on fire. The house burned down with Mom in it. I was ten." He flinched. "Hey! Watch that, will you?"

My little pinky splint scraped his cheek. I stopped petting him and wondered if I should feel shocked, sympathetic, or horrified. "The Mom story," he said. "It's a downer, I know. Hope I didn't ruin your night."

"What's the name of your bike?"

"Lila," he said, snuggling closer to me. After a few minutes of silence, I heard the quiet rattle of a smoker's sleep. And I thought I had a rough time growing up in Short Hills, New Jersey, home of the mall. I kissed his eyelids, slipped from his grasp, and put on my clothes. The pendulum clock on the wall read 4:00 A.M., Friday.

My legs quivered (not just from sex) as I made it down the elevator, no problem. I half expected some nefarious hoodlum to spring at me and thwart my hasty retreat, and I was ready to jab my pinky in his eye. Instead, at the front door, I got Lars. He handed me my coat, gat, and bag and instructed me to wait. I demanded to know why, but he lumbered off into the library without answering. I cursed loud enough for him to hear. I wondered what was going on—perhaps a gift was in store. A horn blasted from outside. I opened the blood-red front doors. On the sidewalk of East 11th Street, straddling the bitchingest hog I've seen this side of Oakland, the man I recognized as Smith Jones waved me over.

Above the varooms, he yelled, "Hop on, babe. I'm your ride home."

I said, "Turn off the bike."

He yelled, "What?"

I reached over and twisted the key. The noise died, and Smith gaped at me. I said, "What, didn't think a girl knew anything about bikes?"

"Where's the gas go, brain machine?" he asked. I pointed to where Peter Fonda hid his drugs in *Easy Rider*. I hoped I wouldn't have to prove myself further—that was all I knew.

"Yeah, yeah, well where's the oil go?"

"Are you lackeys on some kind of schedule? You knew when I got here, knew when I was leaving. Maybe you can count that high—how many orgasms did I have?"

"I'll have to check the videotape later."

"WHAT?"

"Heh, heh. Just kidding, babe. Got you there."

He seemed friendly enough, but I wasn't so sure he was joking. "What's the poop, Smith? Chaperone? Protection—or spy?"

"The full name's Smith Jones. But you can call me anytime." He chuckled. "Heh, heh. Got you again." What a silly-billy.

"You're stoned," I assessed.

"I resemble that remark," he concurred.

"Then you're hungry. Let's go to Kiev." Kiev is the best twenty-four-hour Russian deli/coffee shop in the nabe. Few of the waitresses speak American and the roaches are bigger than Mars bars. Great blintzes. It'd been hours since the duck, and I'd earned an appetite, besides.

Smith said, "I promised Strom I'd get you home safe."

"What, am I some kind of kewpie doll? I can take care of myself, jack. Get out of my way. I'm taking a cab."

"Don't blow my high, babe. I've got a job, just like you." He smiled like Mr. Ed, and his blond ponytail swung. "I drive better stoned." He winked, turned the key, and varoomed madly. I remembered my New Year's resolution to develop a more self-destructive life style. I climbed on the hog, and we blasted off into the once-quiet downtown morning.

We did eighty over the Brooklyn Bridge on the thousand-pound scrap of metal. It must have been twenty degrees, minus fifty with the wind chill. Smith sang "Born to Be Wild," and I screamed at him to watch the road. The grating on the bridge made the bike hum and vibrate. Once we hit asphalt, Smith optioned red lights and stop signs. He whooped at garbage men (they were the only people up) and hastened me to my brownstone in Park Slope alive. I jumped off, careful to avoid the muffler, and asked Smith to see me up. He probably knew something, and in his stoned state, he might spill.

He said, "Whatever you say. But don't come on to me. If I lay one hand on the boss's babe, I'm dead meat." I couldn't help liking the idea of being called Strom's babe.

I examined Smith in his Oshkosh, leather, boots, and spurs. His hair was wild from the ride (we had worn no helmets) and his cheeks were rosy. He was scruffy and adorable, but the sex alert had been answered by Strom only hours ago. I said, "You're too cute to screw, Smith."

"Don't let the overalls fool you, babe. I've killed hundreds."

I let that pass, again, not sure if he was joking. We went upstairs and Smith spread himself out on my cat-stripped couch. Otis trotted over and I felt the usual pang of guilt for leaving her alone so long. She leapt on Smith and licked his face. I spooned out Cheese Bits. I put on water for tea. I excused myself and withdrew to the bathroom. It'd been awhile, and I'd been wary about asking Strom where the ladies room was at the headquarters. After I did my business, I looked in the mirror. My face seemed the same, but I felt different post-Strom—more vital. No bruises were yet visible on my arms.

When I returned to the living room, Otis was milking Smith's gut and he was firing up a fattie. He asked, "What do you call a cow with no legs?"

"Watch her claws. She's vicious."

"Ground beef. Get it? Heh, heh." I walked over

with a hot cup and sat on the couch next to him. I took a hit.

"Thanks," I said. "Tell me about Strom. After spending some time with him, I'm feeling a bit moony. My perspective is shot." I meant it.

"You'll never get me to say a bad thing about Strom Bismark."

I put my hand on his thigh. "I will use sex to get what I want."

"That's something about Strom you probably knew already." He leaned forward and Otis jumped down. He kissed me chastely on the cheek. "I'm off. Strom's a-waiting." Then he split unceremoniously. I could hear the roar of the hog for at least ten blocks. I felt wracked suddenly and lay down on the couch. I wondered if I'd learned anything useful today. I counted back the days from my last period. Slumber flattened me soon after.

It was the kind of morning when I promise myself every fifteen minutes that I'll get up, but I never do until at least two hours have floated by. I spent the time fantasizing about my future as Strom's moll. I wondered if I'd have to get a new wardrobe. I wondered if he'd pay for it.

I forced myself up by noon. The answering machine was blinking. All five messages were Alex. He'd started with a mellow one: "It's nine. Give me a call if you get the chance. No big deal." And ended with an aggravated one: "It's three in the goddam morning. Jesus. Where the hell are you? Call me the second you get in—I mean it, Wanda." Darling Alex sounded a bit jealous. I loved it.

The phone rang while I was getting dressed—501s

and a cashmere sweater. I let the machine pick up. "You've reached the Bowels of Despair. This is your manager, Wanda, speaking. We don't take reservations. Beep." I recorded that during my heartbreak reclusion. It killed me that Alex heard it five times the night before. I made a mental note to change it.

The caller said, "You'd better be on your way over here." It was Alex, presumably at Do It Right. Poor thing, he's probably worried stiff. "Bring money. I want to get paid today." He hung up. I thought about torturing him with ennui on the walk to the subway.

On the platform, I noticed she was there again: the attractively built female pickpocket. I caught her eye, but she ignored me. She was checking men out, as we all do on subway platforms—choosing in the crowd of riders who we'd most like to fuck. The train pulled up and I made sure to board her car and hover nearby. I hid behind an old woman with fifty shopping bags to watch her unreservedly. She waited for easy prey. It wasn't until West 4th Street in Manhattan that a candidate obliviously strolled in.

He had long hair and an attitude, so I assumed he was in the music business. His wallet was in his back pocket, but peeking out just enough for a not-so-innocent jostle and swipe. I looked away from my secretaryish friend for one second to tell the blue-haired old woman to quit poking my back with her bags. When I turned around, the guy's wallet was gone and the chick had boogied down the middle aisle into the next car. Blast, I thought. Missed it. So much for the free subway entertainment. I got off at 42nd Street and jogged over to Times Square.

Alex had cleaned the whole office, which meant he was either in an especially good mood or a particularly bad one. He harrumphed when I walked in. I tried to get him to make eye contact—I'd look away quickly, like I had something to hide. He wouldn't give me the chance. He pointed to a gold locket and chain with a hook clasp on my desk. He said, "That was Flush's. I found it under my couch last night when I was vacuuming. That's why I called you a hundred times, so you can wipe that smug expression off your face. I couldn't care less what you did with Strom." The locket felt solid and heavy in my hand. "There's a picture inside," he said. Indeed, there was. She was a nice black-haired woman in a frilly collar, smiling numbly for the birdie. "Don't thank me, or anything." He glowered at me.

I wondered how the chain could have fallen off her neck and under Alex's couch. While necking madly, no doubt. "Her mom?" I asked.

He shrugged. "She left that at my apartment the night she disappeared. I didn't get around to asking who the woman was." He smirked and pushed hair off his face.

I checked it over for dents and scratch marks, like Columbo would. I said, "You don't have to try so hard to make me jealous, Alex." I picked out the photo with a paper clip. There was no writing on the back.

"Don't do that, Wanda," he warned. "It's a clue."

The office door banged open. The public dicks entered. Detective O'Flanehey twisted his mustache and said, "Cupcake, what happened? Someone shoeshined your head?" He strode over and grabbed the locket. "I couldn't help listening to your conversation with my ear pressed against the keyhole."

"Funny how that works," contributed Detective Bucky Squirrely.

Alex plopped down in the plush client chair and muttered to himself. He'd met these cops before.

"Don't get too comfortable there, beanpole," Dick said to Alex. "We've got a few questions for you."

"Alex is working for Do It Right," I said, "and if he answers any questions, he'll be breaking client confidentiality laws."

"Shut up, cupcake," Dick said. "All right, Beaudine. According to our star witness, you and Flush Royale were closer than ketchup on fries." It sounded like something I would say. "She ran off in a hurry a week before she was killed. I'd bet my bottom dollar she was running from you."

Bucky added, "We know about the fight."

"What fight?" I asked. Alex turned paler than usual.

"The night she disappeared," Bucky started, "Beaudine and Flush were seen arguing on the street in front of the Outhouse. He got steamed and stormed off."

"Want to tell us about it here—or downtown?" Dick always threatened to cart you downtown and he'd accent the word ominously. He waited for a response. I could tell by the look on Alex's face that it'd be a while before he got one. Bucky stared at my pinky splint. Dick twirled the locket on his finger like worry beads.

"Are you paying this star witness?" I asked. "How much does a selective memory go for, these days?"

"We don't pay witnesses, cupcake. Although the person in question may be compensated in some way which I'm not at liberty to discuss."

"Alex will only respond to a sworn statement."

"Wanda," Alex said, "enough with your official-speak. It smacks of bullshit, even to me."

"Then climb out of your own quagmire."

"I don't recall asking for help."

"You never ask. You just brood around all day long until I'll do anything to snap you out of it." I turned to Dick. "He's passive-aggressive. It's so annoying."

Dick and Bucky watched silently as we aired our dirty laundry. So I'm not discreet. "Mind if I interrupt?" Dick asked. "It seems that there was a large sum of money stolen from the safe at the Outhouse a day before Flush's body was found. Our witness has theorized that she was caught in the process of stealing it and ended up losing the money and her life. We're looking for a thief and a killer. Our witness thinks he's in this room."

I gasped dramatically. "Bucky—no!"

Alex said, "It's a smokescreen, Wanda."

"Convincing *her* won't keep you out of the hoosegow." That was Dick.

"The witness, he's involved too?" I asked.

"Nice try, Mallory. No gender has been specified," Bucky leered.

"So, it is a man." My eyes were peeled for a flinch, some indication of admission. Nothing. They train these bastards well at the police academy. "I saw the body. Whoever stroked Flush has got to have a wicked wheelhouse."

Dick twisted his mustache. "You're going in the wrong direction, sweetie. Considering the murder weapon, a ten-year-old with a running start could have done it."

"A ten-year-old couldn't get his fingers around that salami."

Dick and Bucky froze. The locket collapsed midtwirl and fell off Dick's finger onto the orange-as-orange-can-be carpet. I snatched it up and dropped it down my sweater. Dick took a step toward me, and I said, "Don't even think about it."

"No one knows about the salami." That was Bucky.

"No one except little old me."

"And the killer," reminded Dick. "Beanpole here probably told you everything, and you're helping him cover it up."

"Why would I do that?"

"People do crazy things in love. Isn't that right, beanpole?"

Alex, still sitting and avoiding anyone's eyes, said, "Women in love tend to hurt themselves; men tend to hurt others. I'll give you that. The idea that I could hurt someone in love isn't so off," he said, looking at me fleetingly, "but there's also a difference between hurting someone and killing someone. I've never loved anyone enough to kill." I wondered if I should have felt insulted.

Alex rarely misses an opportunity to shoot his sagacity like a cannon—it's one of the reasons I fell in love with him. But the literal, logicalness of it can drive a high-strung emotional gal to the brink. I fought a sudden urge to slap him.

Dick said, "Sounds impressive, but you're still swinging from the hook." He paused. "And I'd like an explanation, cupcake, about how you know about that salami."

"Salami? Did I say anything about a salami?"

"That salami happens to be an old Italian message. It means whoever got it had better come through or he'll be ground and stuffed into a sheepskin. Understand?"

I nodded.

"That should be enough to warn you what kind of trouble you're getting yourself in. And I want that locket back. We're still trying to piece together Flush Royale's past."

"A piece for a piece. Even trade. You'll get nothing from me first."

"Need I remind you who's wearing the badge here?"

"Forget the upstanding citizen speech, Dick. It's tired."

"You want a trade?" he asked. "I'll give you a trade. You hand over that locket, and I won't bust your boyfriend. Today."

"Deal."

Alex's head jerked toward me. He said, "The hell you will. I'll go downtown, up the river, wherever the fuck you want me to go. But she's not giving anything away for free."

Bucky said, "That's not what we heard." He yucked at Dick.

I dug in my bra for the locket and tossed it to Dick. He pocketed it and left with Bucky only after much self-congratulatory revelry.

Alex was furious. He said, "I don't need or want help."

"This macho act. It's not very becoming."

"Now we're down a clue."

"And up a suspect." I didn't mean it.

"It's a good thing I know you're kidding, Wanda. Otherwise, I might get upset." I counted off mentally how I'd hurt myself for him. The months of depression, begging him to come back, even taking this case. Maybe sleeping with Strom. I couldn't help resenting him for a second.

I said, "How long have you known me?"

"I've never known you to fuck up for no reason." I wished I knew that about me.

"Have I ever given anything away before?"

"Detecting 101, Wanda. The case is always more important."

I reached into the pocket of my jeans, and between thumb and forefinger, I flashed him the tiny, yellowed locket photograph of someone's mother. I'd tucked it into my jeans when the cops barged in. "I think it's time we had ourselves a talk, Alex," I said. "If you lie to me again, you are on your own." I would be too, and the idea scared me. He probably had no idea how much the truth mattered.

We said a lot to each other that afternoon, not all of it having to do with the case, and much of it we'd said before. Eventually, we agreed to see how things developed—romantically, that is—and to put off making a decision until the case was over. I hinted that it might be too late by then, and I verbally danced around Strom, but Alex didn't seem threatened. The fight he had with Flush was nothing, but he openly confessed about spending one night with her—he was drunk, she seduced him. I took it badly. That's when I started sobbing. I hadn't cried for him yet, and I figured it wouldn't hurt if he watched. He let me sit on his lap, and he held me. I thought about how weird it was that our sexual/romantic entanglements were wound up in the case. I also thought about how connected I was to Alex. It was like we had the same skin.

He had to go, God knows where, and we agreed to hook up later for the Friday night bacchanalia at the Outhouse. All in all, our talk did little to assuage my baffled notions or reunite us in holy monogamy. I believed he was as truthful as he could be. And I believed he was not the killer or the thief, even though his involvement was growing deeper by the hour. I wasn't sure what to do next.

As Santina said, when in doubt, shop. Thoughts of zipping up the mini churned my stomach. I hopped a cab on Broadway outside Do It Right to go downtown to buy a new one. In the rearview mirror, I thought I saw a gray shark swimming south behind me. When I checked, there wasn't a limo in sight. I got out on St. Marks Place in the East Village, as commercial a street as one could hope to avoid in New York City. Every shop, restaurant, and bar has an enthusiastic name and a colorful awning. A mural of a one-eyed gringo smoking a butt covered an entire building side. The air was cold and wet, but dozens of sidewalk salesmen selling spank magazines clogged easy passage. I picked my way through the dinner crowd of dark, sullen faces steered toward health food joints. The other million people on the street were cramming into bars, smoking on stoops, posing, or enjoying the show—even in January. I stepped on the pointed toe of someone's cockroach killers on my way to the Metro-rama—one of the clothes boutiques from my trendier youth. I apologized and quickly ducked into the shop for new leathers.

Up front, a spiky-haired girl tugged her earring and read *High Times* magazine. She ignored me, so I poked around. Bondage goodies lay innocently in glass cases. More nose rings were available than earrings, and they didn't sell in pairs. On a lark, I tied a studded thong around my good wrist. I could feel my fingers tingle from the cut circulation. I pictured Strom on his bed that morning and remembered the first moment he lowered his entire weight on me. I yanked the thong tighter and reached for where he bit my shoulder. I imagined I could feel the wetness of his mouth. I checked to make sure the salesgirl wasn't watching. I made myself stop thinking about sex and unwound the strap.

The clothes and shoes were in back. I sorted through the minis with side zippers on a circular rack and took three in different sizes to a dressing room. With leather, you can never be sure. The room was an entirely enclosed closet. lacquered on one yellow wall was a life-sized likeness of Marilyn Monroe in her birthday suit. On the adjoining wall was a mirror. The shop designer probably planned it for unavoidable masochistic comparison. I pulled off my jeans and Doc Martens. I liked how my hipbones punched out the sides of my underwear. Strom probably liked that too.

I tried on the medium. I could breathe easily, but it was a bit shorter than Flush's. If I bent over, whoever wanted to could see my ass. I held up my sweater for the side view—my weakest. There was a hint of bulge around the stomach shelf, but nothing a couple hundred sit-ups couldn't fix. I reminded myself that guys like a little meat on the bones. Strom didn't seem to mind. I pulled up my sweater to check for scratch marks. There was one across my ribs. I ran a finger over it.

The dressing room inched open. I jumped and tugged my sweater down. I said with my surliest New York snarl, "Don't you knock?" But it wasn't the salesgirl, hunting for shoplifters.

Gigantor, heaving and near-bald, closed the door behind him. He said, "Open that mouth and lose it, sister." He filled the tiny space and there was suddenly no room to manuever. My bag, with Mama, lay uselessly on the floor, out of reach.

"Look in a biology book if you want to see tits, big guy." The limo had followed me. I cursed myself for not checking twice.

He had one of the leather straps I'd just been admiring in each of his dinner plate hands. He grinned sadistically and lunged. In embarrassingly short order, he tied each of my wrists around clothes hooks on opposite walls. I had to stand on my toes to make the reach. His eyes took a walk all over me. It was as humiliating as being touched. He said, "Don't go away." He threw back his head, laughed, and took his leave.

Abduction, redux. And I thought I'd given it up for Lent. I didn't fight Gigantor off for one simple reason: life may throw you curve balls, but it doesn't mean you have to swing at them. This was one of those times when it's best to ease back and take a pitch. If you're lucky, you'll get a ball. I stopped hacking at curves a while ago. I got tired of going down swinging.

There was a polite knock at the dressing room door. I said, cheerfully, "It's open. Come on in." I wasn't surprised to see the bearded Nick Vespucci in his silk pajamas. He entered the dressing room, Gigantor squeezing in behind him. Saint Nick smiled, showing off his pointy incisors. The smell of garlic was even stronger than before.

"I'm still working on your nickname," he said sweetly.

"Don't knock yourself out."

"Dreadfully sorry about all this," he said, pointing at my wrist. "You know how I hate violence, but I didn't know if you'd talk to me otherwise. Our last adventure didn't end so well for you." He meant my pinky. "Just a little insurance. This horrible city of ours makes people so unruly. You understand. Please forgive me."

"What time is it?" I asked.

His ancient face seemed puzzled. He lifted a skeletal hand and smacked me across the face. Gigantor threw back his head and laughed. The slap didn't hurt, but it was so unexpected that tears popped out of my eyes. He said, "I'm sorry again. Please forgive me." I wondered then if Nick might be a few peas less than a pod. All crazy people have a trigger. It was as good a time as any to find his.

Nick chewed his lip and said, "I'm bored with breaking fingers. I feel energetic today. I'll hit you if you need it. All right? Now, did you give Strom my message?"

"Yes."

"What did he say?"

"He said you were a cocksucker." Nick gasped with delight. "He also said you had something on him, but he wouldn't tell me about it."

"Good. Did he tell you who's in Queens?"

Who? Strom hadn't mentioned a who. I didn't have an answer, so I went digging for Saint Nick's trigger. I said, "Sit on it and rotate."

He smacked me with relish and mustard. It hurt that time. He said, "Did Strom tell you about his mother?"

"Yes."

"He did?"

"Surprised?" I asked.

"I'm surprised a nice girl like you is still working for him."

"That was years ago."

"Not so many."

"He was a kid."

"He still is."

"Tell me about Bisque-Mark, Inc. You fronted for it."

"Hmm. Well, yes. I did give Strom the money for the business. If I were you, I wouldn't discuss that mess with him. He's touchy about it. It was his first failure. And at his age, mistakes mean more. You're still young enough to make mistakes. How old are you again, dear? Twenty-one?"

"Nick, you flirt."

"Hmm. Well. Yes, actually, I am. You can't blame an old man for trying." He rubbed his palms together. "Back to business. Unless Strom is lying to you, and that's entirely possible, the money is gone. I have other sources, who I can't divulge. You understand, I'm sure. Strom hired you to find the money. If he told you about his mother like you said, we both know that I have a personal stake in whether or not Strom can pay up on Sunday. I respect you far too much to ruin your efforts, so I won't detain you. But I want to know what progress you've made. Any luck? Hmmm?"

"You know already. I've got jack."

"Things are good with you and Strom?"

"He pays in advance."

"He's not a bad boy. Misdirected, maybe. A woman like you might be just the thing to straighten him out." He chewed his lip. "I best be off. I hope you won't mind if I leave you hanging. Wouldn't want you to shoot that cute little gun of yours at me. I'm so hungry suddenly. I'd ask you to dinner, but an attractive young woman like yourself must have plans. Farewell, my lovely. And please, forgive me."

Saint Nick walked out first. Gigantor stayed behind,

and he reached for my bad hand. I had a moment of blinding fear that he was going to do further damage, but he just poked the splint to give me a quick jolt of pain. I didn't know if I should thank him or not. He smiled and stroked one of his dinner plates over his bald spot before he left.

As I stood, unshaven and strapped with thongs to the dressing-room walls of a downtown bondage-wear emporium, I indulged in several moments of contemplation. This case was careening out of control. Everyone knew more than I did, and Strom was hardly forthcoming. Getting paid didn't seem enough anymore. I wanted answers and I'd get them, by gum, as soon as I untangled myself. I struggled, but the more I yanked, the tighter the knots got. It occurred to me that Gigantor might have been a sailor in a former life. Maybe he flattened the spiky-haired salesgirl. That I might be completely alone—usually a good thing—burned parts of me I didn't know I had. I was forced to use the one word I promised myself I'd never use unless in mortal combat with flesh-mangling hyenas—

"Help," I screamed.

CHAPTER SIX

Funny as a Crutch

The dangerously tressed salesgirl was wearing my mini. It looked better on her. She eyed me harnessed in the dressing room, shook her head and groaned, "Not again."

"I trust you get an employee discount."

"What is it with you people?"

"Genetic tic," I heckled. She sprung me by scissoring the straps. I had to pay for them—they sell more thongs that way. Once at the register, I forked over my Visa and lowered my lids sheepishly. The straps and mini totaled a cool hundred (dollars, that is). Client expense or not, my card would never cover it.

She dialed the credit people. While she waited, she asked, "Who does your hair?"

Whoever did hers mustn't have gotten his pruning license yet. I said, "Adrienne Argola." That's the name of Santi's salon.

"Yeah, but who?"

"Santina Epstein."

"No way."

"Way."

"I trained with her for my beauty school certificate."

"And you've done so much with it," I said. She didn't hear me. She was reciting my Visa number into the phone. Her black-rimmed orbs flickered over me before she hung up. Here it comes, I thought.

"You're over by twenty," she said, but she handed me a receipt anyway. "Tell Santina that Bermuda Betty says hello." I took the shopping bag and high-tailed before Bets could change her mind. It was still winter outside, but the chilled evening air surprised me for some reason. I gripped my purchase and grinned. That yin-yang thing again. Life has such a persistent way of encouraging me. I made a mental note to give Santina a big wet one.

I made it to the Outhouse dressed in full regalia and on time. It was 10:00 P.M. on Friday night. My subway ride from Do It Right was uneventful. No pickpockets, no one I wanted to fuck. Nonetheless, I felt totally cute. On arrival, I spotted Alex holding down a bar stool in his familiar Michigan varsity and high-tops. I guessed he wears the leather only when he's feeling dangerous. He looked me square in the mini and winked. Billy, the calculator impresario, sunk into the blood-colored curtains, hummed his lunar tune quietly to himself, and tried to be ignored with more effort than was necessary. And Crutch, alias Sally the Post-It girl, was swishing drinks and her hips in more directions than I thought possible. I expected her to nod, smile, give me some indication that we were to rap later about her clandestine message. But she barely glanced at me, and when she did, her expression was one of someone smelling shit. Her vibes were less than friendly. I wondered if she was offended. I wondered how I could have offended her. Intent on finding out, I clicked through the crowd of downtown denizens toward Crutch in my Maude Frizon sample sale pumps. Crip Beluga in a blue-fringed suede and chaps cut me off at the pass.

"Darlin'," he whispered, "you're going to be as lonesome as a lost filly tonight, I reckon. In my office." He propelled me by the elbow, and I registered a thousand eyes upon me. Everyone in the joint had picked me out. I had no idea what I'd done wrong.

Crip slammed the office door. I immediately flashed to Flush's splattered corpse on the cream carpet. I shook it off and focused on the urban cowboy. The swelling in his nose had gone down. I said, "Loving the jacket. It's very neo-pimp."

"You've got more nerve than a blind bullfighter," he blithered. "What in the dang-blazes are you doing here?"

"What, the roulette wheel isn't fixed?"

"The dang-blast wheel is fixed. Sheeit."

"Skirt too short?"

"I could give a horse's patootie about the skirt."

"Autistic Billy have a paranoiac seizure?"

He flitted his eyelids in mock disbelief. He said, "You have no idea what's going on here, do you, darlin'?"

Not a clue. I said, "I know exactly what's going on."

"And you still want to work?"

"I never walk away from a job."

"Then I suppose I can't make you git—you've got, ahem, friends in high places. But if you give a hoot 'n' hollar for me at all, promise you'll stay a Texas mile from Crutch tonight."

The Outhousers had obviously been fed some juicy

information. "Nothing's going on with me and Strom," I said.

"And Ronald Reagan is one of the great thinkers of our generation."

"I like that." I did. Hmm, I pondered. Crip had a habit of reminding me he's not as vacant as a Harlem synagogue. I wondered if Crip was the public dicks' star witness.

He said, "Stay, then. You're moving the hooch." I stopped wondering.

I gently closed the door behind me. He didn't follow—a mistake. There were few men in this world I'd give a hoot 'n' holler for, and Crip Beluga was not one of them. I teetered straight for Crutch, who was flirting with two polyestered gentlemen at the dice table. A Texas mile, my ass. And I certainly had no intention of moving any hooch.

Alex, my sidekick, was winking madly at the bar, trying to get my attention. I waved him off, and he hauled off the stool and marched over. Once close enough, he whispered, "What am I, chopped liver?" He flopped hair off his face with his jungle paw and then arranged his arms akimbo.

"Why is it you always get to places before me?" I asked.

"I like to watch you coming."

"Likewise."

He blushed and said, "Everyone here knows about you and Strom and it makes me want to spontaneously vomit." I was expecting something more heartfelt. I turned to walk away. "Where are you going? Listen to me." He vise-gripped my shoulders and said, "Crutch and Strom are married."

That couldn't be possible. I said, "That couldn't be possible." I touched the hickie on my neck. "She's

111

screwing Crip. I've seen them together. They kiss. They fondle. They coo."

"They're cousins."

I spoke over the rock in my throat. "And how are you privy to this information?"

"Crutch stood on the bar an hour ago and threatened to suck your brains out through your nose."

Gracious, I thought. Sounds painful. That wasn't the worst of it. Strom was a scurvier dog than I imagined. Even someone as unworthy as he was also unavailable. That made *me* want to spontaneously vomit.

Alex rubbed it in. "You are some piece of work, Mallory," he said. "If you could bottle that talent of yours for pissing people off, you wouldn't have to do this for a living."

"Since when were you so articulate?"

"In a fair fight, I'd put money on you, but Crutch is the home team. And," he added, "she's got really long nails. Did you notice?"

My gray cells throbbed. Strom and Crutch were married. Crutch and Crip were cousins. Crip and Strom were, then, cousins-in-law. I guess that secured me a spot on everybody's shit list. And Alex, my angel Alex, was beaming like he'd fucked a light socket.

He said, "I guess this thing with Strom and you is over now, huh?"

"Hold my coat," I said, flinging my Donna Karan over his arm and hanging my bag over his shoulder. "The meter's running."

I couldn't walk too quickly or too authoritatively in my heels. But when Crutch saw me, she squared her spiked feet and eased her massive behind off the dice table. A hush fell over the joint. Some asshole at the bar rearranged his chair to face us and propped a beer on his belly to ready himself for the early evening's entertainment. I'd be damned if I'd end up on the floor. In my mini, the crowd would see sides to me I didn't especially want to show.

Crutch fanned a lethal manicure. She said, "Stop right there, you adulterer." Her lipstick was as sparkly as red could be.

I rebutted, "How was I supposed to know he was married?"

"Yeah, it's not like you're a detective or anything." Her first blow—a below-the-belter. Whoop, whoop, went the crowd.

"I'm sorry, all right," I said professionally. "He doesn't wear a ring."

She exhaled, exasperated. "Did you ask him about the tattoo? Like I told you?"

"We can't talk about that here." A hiss of murmurs from the crowd.

She snorted wickedly and said, "Here's the only place I'll talk."

"The tattoo has nothing to do with you."

"You have no idea what's going on here, do you?" It was the second time in the last ten minutes someone'd said that to me. My inflatable ego wasn't taking it well. "Strom does this all the time," she fired. "He'd fuck mud if it moved."

I reasoned that a professional approach would be to my advantage. I said, "Maybe if you gave decent head, he wouldn't have to." Brain-damage blow. Huge roar from the spectators. Crutch's pretty face contorted with anger. I'd insulted her blowjobs. You can't get more brutal than that.

"You BITCH," she shrieked, and she came at me

113

like a whirling dervish from hell, her talons slicing the air. I had a three-second lifetime to decide to fight back. Maybe if I downed her, I'd gain her trust. Some people are like that. My first move was to dodge her roller coaster. She spun by, but grabbed a hearty handful of my luscious black locks on the way. Unfortunately, my head stayed attached. I had to cry out and hated myself for it. My heels rocked backward and I felt myself groundless. Bouncing off her legs, I hit the deck. I spotted Alex on the way down. Three men were holding him back.

"Cat fight," chanted the crowd.

Better centered on the floor, I latched on to her middle finger and pried my hair loose. I thought I heard a snap. She stumbled a step on her five-inch spikes and plopped down beside me, her ample posterior cushioning the fall. She clawed madly in my direction but missed mainly, except for a rake over my ribs. I didn't feel a thing—never have I been more happy wearing a leather bustier. I attempted my knee-to-the-gut, arms-flung-over-the-head pin position. But I remembered my useless left hand too late, and she threw me off easily. The pump of her legs sent me far enough away to kick off my heels and stand. She struggled to an upright teeter. Suddenly two inches steadier, I took advantage and shouldered her around the middle. We fell again, this time with me on top. I managed to straddle her helpless with her arms twisted behind her back. I planted one hand on either side of her head, pinning her by the hair. She twisted and struggled, but she couldn't break free. I didn't dare move—if I flinched she'd surely claw my eyes out. I flashed to the Loser Cries First fights with the neighborhood kids in Short Hills. Crutch didn't cry, but she did lose. I tasted the first trickle of triumph. Next would come a delicious spurt. I hoped she'd let me enjoy it.

She disappointed me by surrendering limply after only a few seconds. Depriving the victor her smug satisfaction is like robbing someone of a base hit. Crutch looked up at me and said, "We couldn't afford rings." Then she started sobbing. The crowd, sensing the end of things, exchanged bills and high-fives. I rolled off her and checked my face and arms for nail digs. A nick on the collarbone. Nothing more. Still prostrate, Crutch pulled her arms out from under her and covered her face. I noticed her wrenched middle finger and couldn't believe she wasn't in more physical pain than emotional. She sat up. Her bustier had shifted off-center from the fight. On her now-visible left shoulder blade, permanently burned into her flesh, was a dagger-dipped-in-purple-blood tattoo. She sobbed, "At sixteen, we couldn't afford anything."

A mixed fog of realization and excitement sank into my head. She's on the verge of spilling major guts, I thought. I'd finally get to learn something relevant about my employer.

"You've wanted to talk about this for a long time," I prompted.

"My finger hurts." She looked at her hand in a daze.

"You're coming home with me."

"The hell she is," said Crip, looming overhead like a cow balloon. "I'll be hog-tied before she leaves this room. But I advise you," he meant me, "to git the dang-blazes outta here faster than a rattlesnake can bite. And take this lummox with you." He jerked his thumb at Alex, grinning next to him.

"I lost a ten-spot because of you," he said. "I told

you to throw it in the third round." He helped me to my feet as Crip lifted Crutch.

Billy, the casino idiot, dithered over. In his hand, his pocket calculator was glowing. He shoved it in my face. It read: I.SELL.BELLS (57738.7735.1).

I said, "I gave at the office." Alex handed me my shoes and I slipped them on. The altitude rush made me weave, but I soon regained my equilibrium. I turned to Crutch, who was crying on Crip's shoulder. "Are you coming?" I asked. "My upstairs neighbor, the doctor, can take care of your finger."

"Strom promised he'd take care of everything."

"Strom lies," I said. "The sooner you figure that out, the better." I was talking to myself as much as to Crutch. I circled her good wrist with my good hand and yanked her along. She waved off Crip's garble and let me lead her out. Alex stayed behind for insurance. We cabbed to Brooklyn. I prayed to myself that Shlomo would be home. I was correct to sense Crutch would come around to trust me—some women are just burning to talk, but they need information knocked out of them. It must have been a nice change for Crutch to be beaten by another woman. I felt a shudder. I thought of Strom and me the night before and some of the things we did together. I wondered if I needed to be forced into trusting people too. The cab cost eleven smackers, including tip. I was careful to get the receipt.

Santina, fresh out of bed and blonder than usual, lit the pilot light on my stove. She put water on to boil and said, "Betty's a beauty school dropout. I don't care how much she helped you, I refuse to give her that diploma." She put Red Zinger tea bags in two

Dartmouth mugs. "The day I had. I'm organizing a protest at the Korean deli. Fifty cents for a banana? Spare me. I told them to take twenty-five and like it. The nerve—they threw me out." She scratched under her chin. "I hate your hair," she said.

Crutch was upstairs with Shlomo getting her busted finger repaired. I said, "I got laid last night."

"If it wasn't with my nice banker boy, I don't want to hear a word."

"It was good."

"Not a word," she warned.

"That girl upstairs is his wife."

"Listen to me, Ms. Swinger, are you listening? I haven't got time for this today. Those Koreans are giving me such a headache. I can't stand myself, I'm so brilliant with civil disobedience."

"I fucked up, Santina. I guess this means I'm going to hell."

"This broken finger thing? Is this a new trend? Talk about your fashion victims."

"I broke her finger. We got in a brawl at an illegal casino in the East Village." She poured the water and handed me a mug. The tea was too hot to drink. I blew off steam.

She sipped with abandon. "I don't want to hear it," she insisted. "You make this up to disturb me. I know you do. So you can stop right now, Ms. Overflowing Exaggeration. And take off those clothes. You look cheaper than a welfare hotel."

There was a gentle knock on my door. I yelled, "Enter." Crutch zigzagged into my apartment and nearly tripped as Otis raced between her ankles. The splint and bandage on her finger looked just like mine, only bigger. She was in fishnet feet. When she righted herself, she turned her eyes at me. Her gaze belied the soft magic of Valium and she said, "Is Wanda your real name?"

"This is Santina. Remember her? Shlomo's fiancée?"

Crutch lazily tugged up her bustier and didn't offer her hand. "You have a very nice husband," she said.

"Fiancé, dear," Santina corrected.

"Does he have a big one?"

Santi snorted (her display of amusement) from the depths of her plump belly. "He sure does. And he's generous with it."

"My husband is generous with his too," Crutch said, "but with other women." She shook out her hair and she didn't start sobbing, for which I was grateful. I asked her if she'd like to lie down and she said no, she was fine. The conversation lulled. I searched my mind for the right thing to say but came up with jack. Out of her element, Crutch seemed vulnerable. I felt a pang of guilt. We made eye contact, hers were dark blue, and then I darted away, embarrassed. Santina saw an opportunity to come to the rescue, something she had a talent for.

She said to Crutch, "Tell me, dear. When's the last time you cooked your husband a nice pasta dinner with tomato sauce. Not from a jar, I don't care what they say on TV. From a jar sucks. Trust me. I know. Ask Wanda."

"She knows," I said.

"See, I know. Here's what you do: You put on some lingerie. You got a beautiful rear end, and as I always say, if you got it, parade around half-naked. Treat him like he's the most important thing in your life for one night, and then ignore him for three solid days. He'll come begging. Trust me."

Crutch shook her head with drug-induced slo-mo. She said, "I appreciate the advice, but you don't get it. He doesn't love me. He hasn't for a long time. And I don't think I'll be able to flatter, sucker, trick, or threaten him into loving me any more than I could cook him a nice dinner or afford any lingerie." Santina opened her mouth. I could see her mental advice Rolodex flipping in her head. But even she had nothing to offer. I remembered Crutch's note to me: I'm older than I look and smarter than you think. Maybe she was even smarter than that.

"Tequila, anyone?" I asked. I knew I could use a jigger. I simply loathe girl talk sober.

"Maybe I should leave you two alone," Santi said. "You seem like a nice girl. I don't know what you're doing with her." She meant me.

I said, "Leave now, Santina."

"Simmer down, Ms. Authority Complex. I know when I'm not wanted. I'll come and make some eggs tomorrow morning. And dear," she said to Crutch, "don't be too upset. He's just a man."

"He's more than that," she insisted. "Ask Wanda." Santina kissed both of us on the cheek and split. I snagged the bottle of Mescal off the top of my fridge and poured two shots. Valium with alcohol can only make you happy. I figured Crutch could use a shot of the giggles.

I gulped the liquid fire. Crutch followed. I said, "This is more than a little awkward for both of us, Crutch . . ."

"Sally Rosenstein."

"I want you to know that screwing another woman's husband is not something I'd do under normal circumstances."

"It's not for most people."

"And I want you to know that the whole thing was Strom's idea. He doesn't even float my boat." I lied.

"Don't start lying to me, Wanda. I need a friend I can trust. I'm alone in this city. Crip is such a jerk, don't you think?" She made little chortle sounds I took to mean the tequila was working. I sighed and felt less guilty. "Crip's father is a shoe salesman from Hoboken. They live above the Clam Broth House on First Street."

"Great fried calamari," I said, searching for a common taste. Besides Strom, that is.

"Yeah," she said. "I hate seafood." She fiddled with her mini.

I said, "Do you want some sweats?"

"Yeah. And a shower."

I led her to my bathroom in back. She closed the door tight and I poked around for comfy clothes. All my sweats were dirty or crumpled on the floor of my bedroom. The only thing I could find was my red Union suit, with bum flap. I wondered if she'd stretch it out and then kicked myself for being selfish. I laid it out on my bed for her and sat down.

I listened to the piddle-paddle of running water and tried to think. It occurred to me that Strom, poonhound of legend, must have slept with Flush. If Crutch would come after me, talons blazing, it was more than likely that she would go after Flush too. Reach for the first handy weapon, like a frozen salami in the freezer, smash Flush silly, then realize what she'd done. Maybe Crutch was bored with poverty and had stolen the money which, according to New York State law, was half hers anyway. And the message in blood—that'd be a smart way to confuse things.

My concentration broke when she started to sing. I

didn't recognize the song, some old bluesy Billie Holliday number. But her voice—that surprised me. Not only could she carry a tune, but she could lift it, pack it and transport it through the steam like air mail. I wondered if I ever sounded that good in my shower—doubtful, even with the acoustics. The water stopped too soon and so did the singing. I fought an urge to applaud but figured that would be rude. I wandered back into the kitchen to give her some privacy. I banged another shot and fired a smoke. Both tasted swell. I wondered what Alex was doing.

Eventually, Crutch appeared, scrubbed and beautiful in a country-fresh way in my red jumper. Her long black hair left wet spots over each breast. Her nipples popped like turkey thermometers. Without makeup, she looked fifteen, but I knew she had to be older. She said, "Is your water mineral-enriched or soft?"

Beats the hell out of me. "I think it's soft."

"It felt hard and hot." Her eyes misted over for a second, and I figured she was thinking about Strom. She took the final two steps to the butcher-block island in my kitchen and plunked her elbows on it. Her head tilted to one side, and a drop of water from her hair fell in the ashtray.

"Wracked from the Valium?" I asked.

"I've been eating them like candy for too many years to zonk out on one." She stretched just the same. The bum button popped off my suit. "Got a sewing kit?" she said, bending to pick it up. I noticed she wasn't wearing any underwear.

"Forget it." I was getting nowhere with the small talk and buzzed from the tequila. "Look, Sally," I said. "You want to talk. I want to listen. So let's get going. It's already one in the morning." Otis jumped

121

on the butcher block. Crutch absentmindedly stroked her long black tail.

"Pretty cat."

"ASPCA."

"Soft."

"A nice conversation piece."

"And you rescued her from certain destruction."

"I guess."

"Do that for me," she pleaded. I didn't know where to start, so she did. "I met Strom when I was singing in a hole-in-the-wall nightclub in Forest Hills. He's from there. The club was the only place within twenty blocks where you could get a beer and a feel for under twenty bucks. I was underage, but I had a good voice and a big butt, so the manager let me sing. This was sometime in the mid-Seventies. I wore tight microminis up to here and bright orange tube tops. Strom came in and said he was an orphan. I talked to him after my show and took him home to stay with me and my mother. She died recently. Don't say you're sorry, because you didn't know her. She was a bitch, but she was Mom.

"Strom's father left him too and we talked about that the whole first night. He said he was living in a foster home. He got into the club with a fake ID he got at a head shop on Eighth Street in Manhattan." She paused and spilled a cigarette from my pack. She torched it with my gun lighter, coughed, and continued. "When he turned sixteen—he'd been living with me and Mom for a couple months—he said he could legally leave his foster home and move in with us permanently. I'd already gotten pregnant by him. Abortions were legal by then, so I had one at a clinic in Queens. But I didn't want him to move in officially, and I didn't want to get pregnant again unless we got married. My mother loved him. I can't imagine any woman not loving him.

"So we got married at City Hall. My mother was the only witness. He didn't have any friends he wanted to come, and I'd pretty much forgotten about my friends because I wanted to spend all my time with him. We got the tattoos as a lifelong symbol of our wedding day, but I always thought it symbolized that first abortion. A promise from him that he wouldn't forget about it, and that we'd have kids one day.

"I'm not sure how long he knew Lars before he left my Mom's house. All I know is that Lars picked him up on his bike on Strom's seventeenth birthday. I planned a dinner for him. Mom and I had been working on it all day. It hurt me before, when your friend Santina was talking about making him dinner and how nice that would be, how much he'd appreciate it. He's not that way. But how could she know, right? She was just trying to help." Crutch took a long drag off the cigarette and grimaced. She coughed again. I tried to figure out why she smoked if she so obviously hated it.

She continued: "So Strom never came back that night. The dinner was ruined. I honestly don't remember what we made—I'm probably blocking. He showed up a few days later and acted like nothing happened. He wouldn't tell me where he'd been, and I learned fast to stop asking. The times in between him staying home got longer and longer, and after a while he never came back. That was over twelve years ago. A check would come every month like clockwork and Mom cashed it without giving me a penny. I never knew how much money he sent or where he got it."

"But you had a job."

"Not for long. I tried to get something going with

123

my singing career until my lymph nodes got infected from breathing wrong. That happens to a lot of untrained singers. Now I can barely speak."

"You sounded hot in the shower," I said.

"You should have heard me back then. I sent a demo tape once to an A&R guy from Columbia Records who saw me at the club. I fucked him, but he didn't sign me. So he fucked me. No tragedy. Everyone is looking for what they can get, why not him? I sound so cynical. I'm not really that way." She put out her cigarette. I felt relieved, for some reason.

"Hooking up with Strom again after all these years started about two months ago," she said. "Crip's mother, my mom's sister, called up to say how her son was rolling in dough. Sisterly competition, Mom said. I wasn't spared the what's-wrong-with-you, you-never-amounted-to-anything lecture. At the time, I was ending a two-year affair with a restaurant owner from Flushing. I had nothing to look forward to, nowhere to go, so I called Crip's mom under my mother's nose and got his phone number. I asked him for a job, and he said he couldn't hire me until someone else quit. Besides that, he felt funny bringing in a relative. I thought, well, there goes that shot, and stayed with Mom. I was really depressed. There was nothing left for me there. Mom was getting more and more crazy about what a loser I was, and I was packing my bags to get out, when she got hit by a cross-Island bus on the way to the supermarket. I had to arrange the funeral and cremation. Selling the house paid off her debts, and I was left with about five grand to my name. And I still had nowhere to go.

"I called Crip again, and out of sympathy, he said he'd ask his boss if he could hire someone part-time for when other girls got sick. I had no idea that the boss was Strom. He changed his name when he founded Blood & Iron, which was one of the reasons I could never find him when I looked."

"His real name?"

"Morris Blechman," she said. "I used to call him Baby Mo-Mo."

I nearly choked. "You're joking," I said, smiling.

"You think that's funny?" She seemed insulted.

"He's such a Strom."

"No one's such a Strom. It's made-up. It's bullshit." She had a point. It occurred to me that that was part of his fascination. He's all persona, no person. He's a figment of his own imagination. A self-manufactured legend. No wonder he protects his image so strenuously.

But I couldn't understand why Crutch seemed protective of him. She got dumped in a ton-of-bricks way. No self-respecting jiltie has that much tendresse. In an effort to get her off the defensive, I changed the subject (although it killed me to). I said, "So Crip hired you after your mother died."

"Not right after. Strom told him he couldn't afford another salary. I got pissed off. Crip was saying all the time how loaded this Strom character was, that the office safe was busting open with cash. I couldn't believe how fucking cheap he was if he was that rich. But the rich ones are the cheapest. I cooled off, and a month later, I got a call from Crip. One of the girls was giving him a headache, could I come in? I said hell, yes. He said it would be easier if no one knew we were cousins, so we pretended to be girlfriend, boyfriend. That's why he called me Crutch. That's what he calls all his girlfriends."

"And what's Crip's real name?"

"What do you mean?"

"What do I mean?"

"Crip Beluga is his real name." This I couldn't believe. I suddenly wondered if her whole story was hogwash. I must have looked doubtful, because she sighed and proceeded to explain Crip's curious moniker. "He was born so bowlegged, his parents didn't think he'd ever walk normally. So they named him Crip. I guess that sounds sort of sick."

"No, perfectly normal." He never looked bowlegged to me.

"He grew out of it," Crutch continued. "His legs are totally straight now. His mother gave him a complex about it even though no one else even noticed. She always said that he walked like he just got off a horse."

"The cowboy thing."

"Bingo."

"Amazing."

"It's semi-psychopathic. I'm used to it by now. It seems normal to me. Anyway, I went in and started working. The girl who was giving him the headache turned out to be Flush. He seemed to want to get rid of her. I don't know why. I got my first look at Strom the second night. I almost had a heart attack. He looked exactly the same, like he hadn't aged a day. I fell back in love with him on sight, just like when I was a teenager. He walked up to me, and I was shocked how he reacted."

"Intense passion? Screaming fight? Feigned indifference?" I queried.

"He didn't recognize me. He even hit on me. He said he had a bigger dick than Crip and that I should check him out that night."

"The bastard." I meant it. "Then you flashed the tattoo."

"I took him up on his offer and he found it himself.

He got mad and asked how I tracked him down. He was convinced I was after his money. He said he should have divorced me years ago. What kind of nightmare was this that I turned up? Forget the money, he said. Forget the marriage. I said, what about the checks? If you didn't care about me, why'd you send money? He said he didn't know a thing about that, and if I was on the payroll it wasn't because of him. I'd never actually seen any of the checks and I thought that maybe they never came. I got confused. Maybe my mother lied so I'd stay with her. I didn't know what to think. He warned me not to reveal his past. But I don't know anything anyway—I only lived with him for a year, and he's not the most talkative guy in the world. Seeing him again—and being with him—was painful, but the way he talked to me was so cruel."

"So you said fuck you, got dressed, and got the hell out."

"He tied me to the bed and slapped me while he fucked me."

"The bastard." I really meant it.

"I asked him to." She read the puzzled expression on my face. "That's what makes me come. What makes you come, Wanda?"

Any number of things too sordid to describe in detail here. "Tenderness," I said. "A soft touch on the cheek. Accidental brushing. A gentle breast caress."

"Bullshit," she observed correctly. "I read you as the kind of woman why could use a slap in the face."

"Maybe you should read the newspapers instead. You might learn something." Discussing my sexual proclivity with the wife of the man I'd spent the previous night with did not sit comfortably with me. (But at a bar with a stranger, I might draw some

127

illustrations on a cocktail napkin.) Don't get me wrong, I fell off my high horse in kindergarten. But no matter how many men I screw in however many pretzeline contortions, I still think of sex as sacred— to be shared and discussed (at length, as it were), but it should not be maligned. I got the feeling Crutch wasn't nearly as curious about my sexual antics as she wanted to show off. Just for the record, I have never been tied up, slapped, and fucked.

"I do read the papers," she said.

"Whatever. Look, Sally. You wouldn't be sobbing this tearjerker if there wasn't something in it for you."

"Are you asking me what I want?"

"As politely as I know how."

"I want what you want."

"Your own talk show?"

"I want to get Strom."

"Get him back."

"Get him. Burn him. See him crumble."

"Then I don't think we want the same thing."

"Sure we do. You just don't know it yet." Whatever she meant by that, she didn't elaborate.

"So why'd you fuck him? And if you hate him so much, what do you care what I do with him?"

She ignored it. "I'm tired. Is it OK if I sleep over?"

"Take the bed," I said, and she wandered down the hall. Her butt, visible and swishing, disappeared a full two seconds after she did.

I got an extra blanket and pillow out of the closet in the bathroom. I felt sloppy and realized that I'd had about five shots in the last hour. I'd have a hangover for sure—job hazard—but I'd sleep better. I arranged my covers on the couch, flicked off the lights, and climbed under in my clothes. It was about three on another frosty January night in Brooklyn. Otis leapt on me and milked me with her paws. After padding down my stomach bulge by marching in a circle, she mewed tiredly and collapsed. In seconds, she was happily snoring her little cat snores.

I waited for sleep and thought about death. There are three reasons people need to kill: sex (love as a subcategory), money, and reputation (to keep or make). If Strom and Flush had a thing going, Crutch might kill her for at least two of those reasons. She had the opportunity: she was working at the Outhouse by then and had access. I wondered if Crutch and Strom had been screwing this whole time or if it was just a one-shot deal. It occurred to me that I might be under the same roof with a killer. Suddenly, sleep was out of the question. I stared at my ceiling, and using my X-ray vision (another cool thing about me), I scanned for spider webs. I counted my breaths and willed myself to sleep.

I wasn't under for five seconds, when the phone rang. Shocked out of limbo, Otis dug her claws into my ribs. I groaned and fumbled for the living room extension. I answered, "This better be good."

"Wanda." Alex. "Get up. We've got trouble."

I said, "This is the answering machine. Leave your name and take a number."

"I know it's you, so cut out the cute shit."

"Are you saying I'm not cute?"

"Jesus."

"Why'd you go out with me if you didn't think I was cute?"

Alex didn't dignify my question with an answer. He stated flatly, "Crip Beluga is dead."

CHAPTER SEVEN

Little Things Spleen a lot

I wrestled with the covers and fell off the couch. I'd been winding up on the floor too often lately. I screamed, "You were supposed to watch him. You were supposed to keep him out of trouble."

"So it's my fault, then?" Alex asked. "If Crip were really dead, I might be miffed at an accusation like that."

"You might be WHAT?"

"Now that I have your attention . . ."

"Fuck my attention."

He said, "You know we can't discuss anything like that until after the case."

My blood careened through my veins. I was more than a little angry. I said, "Fleecing offends me, Alex." Unless I do it, of course.

"I was lonely. I wanted to hear your voice."

"Fuck my voice."

"If you insist."

"Vlad the Impaler? My uncle. We called him Uncle Vladdy."

"I didn't know that."

"Yeah. Family secret. Don't tell anyone."

"Look out your window."

"What's that supposed to mean?"

"Living room window."

I found my glasses in my bag and walked over to the sill. The tall, thin figure across the street at a pay phone waved. I'd know that Michigan varsity anywhere. And that body. I said, "I can't believe it. They still haven't taken down the Christmas lights on Flatbush."

"Crip is missing," he said as I watched him pull his coat tightly around his waist and huddle in the booth. "I have no idea if he's dead or not. It's entirely possible he is. If you want the story, you'll have to let me up."

Three months ago, he could have let himself up. He'd mailed me my keys without a note. "So, you want to come in, do you?" I asked. "You think you can just show up here uninvited, like junk mail?"

He sighed. "If you plan on having one of your episodes, can't I at least watch?"

"Remember what I used to make you do?"

"Wanda, it's freezing out here."

"When I gave you head."

"My fingers are falling off."

"And then I'd stop in the middle. What did I make you do?"

"This is embarrassing."

"Nothing's embarrassing at four in the morning."

"You made me beg for it."

"The exact words."

"Wanda, in five seconds, if I'm not roasting by an open pilot light, I'm going back to the city to look for Crip alone. Do It Right can reimburse me for the cab."

"Cheap bastard."

"Just poor," he said. "I'm so broke I even can't pay attention."

"This attention thing again."

"Four seconds." He hung up. I would have preferred being furious with him for interrupting my (nonessential) beauty sleep, but my girlish excitement could not be thwarted. Alex and me. In my apartment. At night. He didn't have to come all the way out to deepest, darkest Brooklyn—he could have called more easily from the office, anywhere. It was a gesture of undeniable significance, a gesture I could not ignore. I ran to the bathroom and ate toothpaste, dropped my glasses on the kitchen table, and glided out to open the door. (We don't have electronic spring buzzers in Brooklyn. That, and no cable.)

Alex was waiting with an adorable smile. His hair was tousled and all over his face. The street light behind him haloed his head, and I thought for a second that I might die. He said, "Fancy meeting you here."

I used my sexy voice. "Come on up. I'll make tea."

"Do you have a cold?"

"No, you idiot." I turned and stomped up the stairs. My sexy voice was working as well as roach spray. I was still wearing my Outhouse outfit. Alex walked up behind me and I suddenly felt self-conscious. I fought an urge to cover my rear with my hands. We went into my apartment, and Otis, the scoundrel, leapt lovingly into Alex's arms. And people say animals have no memories. He kissed her little face and they headbutted each other. Their special game. I felt nauseated and realized I was not ready to handle the familiarity of this so soon. Plus, I was overwhelmed by an irrational jealousy for my cat.

I said, "You stand over there." I directed him

behind the butcher block. I walked to the heart of the living room, ten feet away. A safe distance. I nervously started humming a tune I didn't even recognize.

Alex said, "Ah, the 'Fatto per la Notte di Natale.' Il Divino."

"And your mother wears army boots."

"No, Wanda. The song you were humming."

"What of it?"

"The *Christmas Concerto*. In G minor."

"Since when did you know anything about classical music?"

"I picked it up. Here and there."

"Maybe there, but not here." I wondered if he learned that at Flush's place.

He poured himself a shot of Mescal. I could tell from the lipstick mark it was my glass. I felt an irrational jealousy for the tequila. Alex made a love it/hate it sound. He filled another shot and licked his lips in anticipation. His throat muscles stretched. He opened his mouth to swallow the fireball, and I thought for a second that I was already dead.

"Stop that," I barked and he looked at me strangely over the glass. "I mean, don't get drunk."

He downed it, raked his hair back, and said, "It has become obvious to me that Strom Bismark not only knows who I am, but that he hates my guts with every fiber in his being." I pondered how Strom could possibly care who Alex was, let alone have a reason to hate him. "He stepped on my foot." Alex held up his Converse and pointed to a nonexistent scuff mark.

I had nothing to say. Alex meditatively rolled the shot glass on top of the butcher block. I said, "Put that in the sink."

"It's not like Strom's my hero or anything—I realize he's no friend to society," Alex said. "But I always wanted to meet him. Now that I have, I'm not sure what to think."

I said, "Tell me everything, and don't leave anything out."

"Why are you dressed?" he asked.

"Does it offend you?"

He shrugged as if the state of my non-nakedness mattered not at all to him. I hoped he was disappointed. He said, "Here's what happened—you and Crutch left, and right after, Crip mumbled random curses and buckaroo slang. He pushed me aside and went into his office."

"You followed him."

"No. I waited for him to come out. When he did, he looked panicked. He went to the bar and told the bartender to make him a double Cuba Libre. He drank. I didn't sit next to him, because he hates me. I'm not very popular at the Outhouse. Then again, neither are you." He snorted.

"You could have provoked Crip into spilling."

"No, not this time. It wouldn't have worked. He was deep, deep into his own head. Other people tried to talk to him but he'd have none of it. About an hour later, Lars came in. I think he was just checking things out to make sure the coast was clear for Strom. I couldn't imagine who Strom wanted to avoid. You and Crutch had already left, and if Crip called him from his office as I'd assumed, Strom would know that. Lars sat down next to Crip and whispered in his ear. Crip's face went white. I moved closer to try to listen. But Strom came up the stairs and everyone focused on him."

"Mother of pearl." I thought of what Crip said about Strom once—that he had magical powers.

"I tell you, Wanda, it's weird," Alex commented. "Strom didn't even say anything. It was like everyone sensed it when he walked in. *I* sure did. I wasn't even watching the door, but I knew something about the room had changed." I felt an ego rush. After all, not every girl gets to fuck a human magnet.

I asked, "What was he wearing?"

"Who?"

"Strom, bonehead."

"I don't know. Pants, a shirt."

"His leather jacket?"

"What jacket?"

Men have no clothes memories. "Forget it."

Alex seemed puzzled. He asked, "Does it matter?"

"It helps to visualize the scene."

"Fine, Wanda," he sneered. "Strom was wearing whatever he wears in your fantasies." In my fantasies, he's not wearing anything. Alex continued, "So Strom walked up to Crip and whispered something. These guys, they whisper. They don't talk like normal people. So Crip shook his head and said, 'She doesn't know anything.' I assume he was talking about Crutch. Then he said, 'She's a woman,' as if that explained something."

"What, as in 'she's nuts'?"

"Hey, I didn't say it."

"They could have been talking about me, brainiac."

"Then they'd be right."

"Are you saying I'm nuts?"

He held up his hands. "What the hell is wrong with you?" he asked. "I'm talking about the case here, how we make money. Do you think you can reign in your ego for ten seconds?" He sighed. "I realize this is a difficult time for you, and I appreciate that your emotions might be clashing at the moment. But snap out of it. You are being paid to solve a crime, not participate in a heavy-metal soap opera."

"You're in this just as much as I am."

"Am I a mass of conflicting impulses?"

"No, you just inspire that in others."

He stared at me blankly. Maybe working with Alex again was the wrong choice. He made me make mistakes. I wondered if Alex was thinking the same thing as he leaned back against my fridge and crossed his arms over his chest.

I said, "Did I interrupt?"

"Wanda, maybe I should . . ."

"Pray, continue."

He sighed and then went on. "While Strom was talking, Crip couldn't look him in the eye. So he couldn't help looking in my direction. We made contact and I winked. His face soured and Strom noticed. He turned toward me and then immediately back to Crip and whispered something. Lars came over and sat next to me. Have you noticed? Lars wears my cologne." I had—and I didn't find it consoling. "Lars smiled at me, and for a second, I got nervous. Then Strom walked over. He said, 'Alex, right?' I said yeah, Alex Beaudine. Strom said, 'You a friend of Wanda's?' I said, yeah, a friend. He said, 'How's she doing?' I said you were just fine. He said, 'Seeing her much lately?' And I said, yeah, every day, we work together. And then he said . . ."

"You told him we're working together."

"He should know. He's footing the bill."

"The shoe incident?"

"That was when he walked out. He passed by me and by-accident-on-purpose stepped on me."

"Slick."

"He's your boyfriend." My jaw dropped. Alex said, "Close your mouth." I glared. "So then Strom said it was a pleasure to meet me and that I should come to the Outhouse anytime."

"The exact words."

"Pretty much that. He was so polite, so nice. He hates me, I can tell."

I asked, "And beyond your paranoic delusions?"

"He told Crip to have his shit together in a half an hour. Then he left with Lars."

"Get his shit together before what?"

"Any ideas?" I shook my head. Alex continued, "Two minutes after Strom left, Crip jammed into high gear. He emptied the cash register, told the bartender to double charge and ran out. I followed in hot pursuit, but I lost him around St. Marks and Avenue A. I looked around and then started back to the Outhouse when I heard the shot."

"Which you assume on a Friday night—in the East Village, where no one ever gets shot—is that this particular bullet may or may not have killed or maimed Crip Beluga at three in the morning."

"Maybe it's a little farfetched." He made his ain't-I-a-lovable-dope smile. It didn't work.

"Alex, what are you doing here?" I asked.

"Working the case."

"Did you go to the B&I headquarters?"

"I came here."

"Why would Strom know who you are?"

"Maybe Smith Jones told him about me. About my book."

"Bull. Strom wouldn't give a shit about that, except to make sure he wasn't in it. Who knew we worked together?" Alex lowered his long lashes and rolled the shot glass on the butcher block again. He stopped mid-circle and put it in the sink.

"You told Flush, didn't you?" I asked. "You told her all about me. You were lying in bed, enjoying the peaceful afterglow. She—being what, twelve?—asked about your past romances. You said, yeah, there's this chick I used to go out with. Her name's Wanda and she carries a gun. Yeah, you said, I dumped her when it got too heavy. Hey, I couldn't take that kind of pressure. Women, you said. She cuddled closer and you kissed on the lips. You told her she was the only girl for you and fucked her again real slow. You make me sick."

"I didn't tell her I dumped you. I said it was mutual."

I said, "You filthy liar." He seemed angry. Never one to make a scene, I changed the subject. "Where is Strom now?" I asked.

He said, "You're a real shit, Mallory."

It wasn't the curse word that got me, but a panic of some kind wrapped itself around my spine like a serpent up a tree. Something was dreadfully wrong. It was a vibe thing. Or maybe it was the way Alex looked at me like he hated me. I had to get out. I reached for my coat on the kitchen stool. The collar got caught and the chair crashed to the floor. I scooped it up and pushed my arms through the sleeves.

"I have to find Strom," I panted.

"You mean Crip."

"Fuck Crip," I blurted. Alex started to speak. "Don't even think about saying it."

"I'm coming with you," he said.

"The hell."

"I'm a free person. I can go wherever I want."

"When you graduate second grade, give me a call." I slipped on my heels. They were the only shoes handy.

Alex crossed the room, cutting the safety distance to none. He pushed me down on the couch and sat on me. He'd gained weight. I tried to push him off, to no avail. I'd forgotten how strong he was. "What are you afraid of?" he asked.

"What makes you think I'm afraid?"

"You're making the O face." My eyes and mouth get round when I get antsy. It's reactive.

I snarled, "How dare you think you know me so well?"

"I dare."

"Then you know how pissed off I am."

"At me?" I nodded vigorously. "I'm on your side."

"Strom knows we're working together now."

"That's a problem?"

"For one thing, lover boy, you're a suspect."

"And you're not? The girlfriend of the man who broke your heart?"

"That's absurd."

"No more than my killing her."

"I doubt Strom sees it that way."

A voice from the hallway said, "He doesn't give a shit about either of you. He just wants his money back." It was Crutch, up from bed. The stool crash must have woken her. I'd forgotten about her, what with all this excitement. Alex jumped off my lap. He had forgotten we weren't alone too.

He said a bit too loudly, "I hope you two wildcats made nice." She yawned. I watched his eyes travel the scenic route over Crutch in my red one-piece. He'd seen it on me and he couldn't hide registering the difference in our bodies. For the first time ever, I felt a crushing dislike for Alex. Not out of irrational jealousy. It had to do with his appraisal of a thinly sheathed female form—mine or Flush's or Crutch's —that consisted of inspection, followed by a flash of dismissal, or acceptance. He appeared to dismiss Crutch. She was clearly too old for him.

I said, "Crutch, go back to bed."

"Is Crip all right?" she asked, and I wondered if she cared.

Alex said, "He's fine. Don't worry." The man taking control.

"I have to leave. Alex, stay and watch Crutch."

"I don't need protection," she insisted.

"I have a sneaky feeling that you do. Sorry. Don't mean to upset you."

Alex asked, "Where are you going?"

"Away."

"I'm coming. Crutch can go up to Santina's."

"Santina is not on the payroll, and I'd rather go bathing-suit shopping than get in a cab with you."

Alex knit his brow—a feigned concern. I felt a wave of disgust. I said, "Why don't you try helping me instead of hurting me for once?"

"It's your show," he said coldly. Crutch yawned, stretched, and went back into my bedroom. Alex watched her go. The bum flap gaped and her butt was visible. We were alone again, and Alex walked slowly toward me—I could tell he wanted to say something he thought was important.

I didn't give him the chance. "I'll call you," I said and split like a banana.

I cried in the cab. No mascara ran. I never wear it; I'm not a mascara person. My tears were more out of frustration than anything. The Alex-and-Strom demolition team were wreaking havoc on my heartstrings, and it occurred to me that I needed a friend. A woman. Someone who wouldn't fuck me or fuck me over. Santina was fine, but she mothered too much. I needed someone more sisterly. I wondered how one embarked on meeting people in this coldhearted city. Heartbreak capital of the world. I tried to think about the case. I lit a cigarette. It tasted swell. The cabbie coughed one time too many and I told him to shut up and drive.

Long rides into Manhattan, in the wee hours or otherwise, force the analytical girl thing. I certainly do not invite moments of contemplative reflection, but they have a surreptitious way of ambushing me. My first quandary was whether or not rushing to Strom was such a good idea, considering that I never trusted him, and now he couldn't trust me anymore because he knew about Alex. My second quandary was that I might be looking for trouble after that emotionally frothing encounter with my clay-footed ex-boyfriend, to punish myself for not being nice. I wondered what I'd resort to in this hell-bent mood. And I must confess that exploring the depths of my self-destructive nature got me more than a little excited. Blue moods usually ended for me at the bottom of a bottle or between rumpled sheets. I flashed to some of the things Strom and I did the other night. Any guilt I'd previously felt about Crutch slid away the farther I got from my apartment. By the time I got to the B&I headquarters, I had only one clear idea of what to do. And it wasn't about staring into the end suds of a dirty glass.

Smith Jones, funnyman, was shining his exhaust pipes outside the graffitied building on 11th and First Avenue. Otherwise, no one was around but some homeless people on the corner and random East Village riffraff. Smith's ponytail bobbed as he bent over, and his overalls fit as tightly as caramel on an apple. When he saw me leap out of the cab, hell-driven to find his fearless leader, Smith dropped his rag and rushed over to greet me. Or to head me off. I wasn't sure.

I said, "Get out of my way."

He said, "Where's the fire, babe?"

"It's ten degrees and I'm in a mood."

"Just answer this first. Why did the Siamese twins move to England?"

"Don't you have a date to pummel someone?"

"So the other one could drive. Heh, heh." He threw his head back to laugh, and I noticed the locket and chain encircling his sinewy neck.

"That's an awful nice necklace you got there, Smith," I cooed. "Where ever did you find it?" From my pals the public dicks, perhaps? I might have discovered the identity of their star witness.

"A friend asked me to wear it. Who am I to say no?"

"Does your friend, perchance, carry a badge?"

"My friends don't need no stinking badges."

"But they need baths."

He sniffed his armpits. "If I gave away all my secrets," he said, "I'd lose my sex appeal."

"Look hard and I'm sure you'll find it."

"Basically, babe, I won't tell because you want to know."

"How chivalrous of you."

"Don't let the locket fool you. I've chivaled hundreds." I jotted that information in my mental steno and walked past him toward the headquarters entrance.

He called after me, "I was going to wear my

camouflage shirt today—but I couldn't find it. Heh, heh." I kicked the blood-red doors open. Lars was on the other side, his massive body propped on a small wooden chair. He looked up like he'd been expecting me. He was doing the *Times* crossword puzzle.

"Don't you criminals ever sleep?" I asked, already knowing they do that during the day.

Lars gestured toward the library. "He's not here."

"Where is he?" I asked, but Lars ignored it. I tried to rile him. "You look like an overstuffed doorman."

"And you look like an undersexed hooker," he commented without glancing above my knees. It was the largest combination of words I'd ever heard him utter at one time.

"I'm going in."

"No, you're not."

I yanked Mama from my bag and planted it in his ear. He didn't even flinch. "Just try and stop me," I threatened with my usual dramatic flair. I waited for a movement. He could have knocked me out with his eyelash, but nothing. He continued filling in the white squares with a red pen. I swept into the library.

The room was black as blood and rank as sweat. The scent of roast duck and zucchini boats from our romantic soiree was no more. Strom had to be nearby. I sensed him. No point in searching, I figured. I decided instead to draw him out by ransacking the joint. Or at least shoot off the handle of the hidden door behind the drapes with my trusty Mama. With some luck, I might uncover a secret ritual room designed for human sacrifice. And if anyone dare try to stop me, I'd just tell them Lars made me do it.

I attempted to flick on the sconces, but nothing happened. I wondered if the long-anticipated electrician had finally arrived to fix the chandelier and switched off the room's current. Damn, I thought. I'd have to do it in the dark. Not my style.

I fumbled in the blackness for the mysterious passage. Once I located it, I lifted my gat lighter from my bag, Mama already in hand. I aimed both heaters at the locked knob, one for light, and one for fire. I squeezed the trigger and the door blasted open. I waited a count of ten for Lars to hurl in and interrupt my progress. Nothing. My heart pounded louder than the U.S.C. marching band. I kicked off my pumps and intrepidly forged down a long, cold, dark corridor, the glow of the butane lighting my way. It was plushly carpeted. There was nothing on the walls except fluorescent yellow arrows aiming toward the black center. My pinky splint scraped against the concrete wall, and it made a spine-shuddering echo. I didn't spot the end door of the secret cul-de-sac until I was almost upon it. And when I did, the aroma of raw curiosity enticed me ever forward, even though I knew barging in wouldn't be the polite thing to do.

From the weight of one step closer, the door creaked open. It was wood and had a nice brass knob. The crack showed me nothing but the soft orange light of a warm room. I sensed no human presence so I leaned forward and pushed the door inward, revealing a studio-sized lair with a stand-up chalkboard square in the middle. To the left was a bed with a stuffed blue comforter from Bloomingdale's ($250 minimum), a dust ruffle, and huge fluffy pillows with laced covers. Clothes were neat in piles on an imposing studded leather chair in the opposite corner. The matching ottoman had been rolled across the room and left in front of the chalkboard. An IBM clone laptop lay dormant on a plain plastic stand. I debated the gender of the space's inhabitant. And the age. The lamp on the night table was left on and the ice cubes in the glass next to it had nearly melted. I scanned around for closets, a bathroom, a hiding place. There were no windows. The room was underground. I dropped my lighter into my purse to free one hand.

I searched the main room for clues silently with my eyes. But all I came up with was that the clothes were masculine and the handwriting on the chalkboard—mathematical formulas—was feminine, almost loving. Due to the lack of visible personal items, I guessed that the resident hung out infrequently or was possibly just visiting. Or had deserted the space in a hurry. The last time I saw logarithms, I was failing eleventh grade math. I had to give the kid next to me lunch money to cheat off her tests.

I eased into the room. The first side door was a closet, no one inside. It was almost empty, except for piles and piles of printed out computer paper covered with numbers. It seemed to be an inventory list of some kind, an ascending pattern of five-digit numbers was clear, but there were no words to explain. A few rumpled suits hung on wire hangers. Even the dandiest one was cheap and short. On the floor, hidden behind a stack of paper, sat a black lead bust of a flamboyantly dressed middle-aged man with pretty ringlets and a Roman nose. The plaque read Archangelo Corelli. Sounds Italian, I thought. The name and face rang no bells.

I moved on. The second closet was shelved and full of clean linen in the same neat, immaculate stacks. Alex's closets challenged these in anal retentiveness. Maybe he should have come along to give a sympathetic psychological profile. I continued to the bathroom.

The door opened outward, and I nearly knocked

myself in the forehead. I flicked the light switch and mentally readied myself for battle. No one. Not in the shower, perched on the toilet, or under the sink. I shook out my adrenaline rush and strode cockily back to the bedroom. I hadn't found another way out, and I was safe for the time being. But if someone caught me, I'd be a dead duck.

I reached to close the bathroom door after me. A hairy male hand groped out from behind it and snagged my bad wrist. It was still sore from the Nick incident, and the pain was immediate. With my other hand, I flailed with my gun and kicked the door closed to see my attacker. But before I could focus (I wasn't wearing my glasses), he'd spun me around and pressed my back against him. He clinched me with one arm around my waist and his other hand entwined in my hair. My ears throbbed from the grip, and he only drew me tighter when I struggled. He said, "What are you doing here?" But the voice wasn't what gave him away.

"I'd know that hard-on anywhere," I said. "Strom, honey, I had no idea you missed me so much."

"You shot my door."

"Lars made me." I lied.

"Don't fuck with me, Wanda."

"Don't you fuck with me."

"How is it you forgot to tell me you hired Beaudine?"

"How is it you forgot to tell me you're married?" He loosened his grip after that, and I was able to face him. "Is that a frozen salami in your pocket?" I asked.

"No." He didn't get it. "Wait, what do you mean?"

"You've got to learn to take a joke, Strom, honey."

"When you say something funny, I'll laugh."

"Look," I said, "all we seem to be doing here is

upsetting each other. Let's sit down. Be mushy. Gushy. We can explain things." I walked over to the bed and plopped down. It wasn't a come on. My legs were still shaking from the struggle.

He asked, "Got cigarettes?" I nodded. He sat next to me and I gave him one. He used my still-hot gun lighter and stoked. I marveled at the way he kept his mouth slightly open when he inhaled. I could see his tongue.

I said cheerfully, "How was your day, dear?"

"What did Sally tell you?" He made tiny circles on my shoulder with his fingertip. I tried to concentrate.

"She said she likes to be tied up and slapped."

"What did she say about me?"

"That is what she said about you." Strom put the cigarette to my lips and I pulled a drag. He fanned his other hand over my shoulder blades and pushed me into it. When I wanted to stop, he wouldn't let me up for a split second too long. I blew out smoke and faced him. His green tornado eyes churned wildly, and I felt a mixture of fear and wetness.

I said, "Why didn't you get a divorce?"

"I'd have to go through the Queens court system, and I didn't want to."

"Because someone would find you."

"Something like that."

"Who?"

"That has nothing to do with the missing money."

"Which is all you really care about."

"Is that what Sally said?" I lied and said no.

He said, "Let me tell you something about Sally and her mother. I was a kid, trying to get over what happened to my house and my mother. And I meet this girl, she lets me fuck her. And she's got a good-looking mother who does too. It was great until they started fighting for me. Flipping quarters for who gets to fuck me next. I didn't like that, so I left. I forgot about them. But Sally never did, and she won't ever. Her mom's dead and now she's blaming me."

"Jeez. It's not like you ruined her life or anything."

"She wants my money or she'll tell the newspapers who I really am."

"I thought the money's for Nick."

"It is." He dragged smoke. If Sally really wanted to crush him, she'd have to do more than demand money. Maybe she knew he was in a pickle with Saint Nick. And if she did, it'd be a swell idea for her to make sure Strom couldn't pay back by emptying the Outhouse safe.

"Does she know about Nick?" I asked.

"I don't know."

"And is protecting your image worth that much?"

"Yes," he said honestly, and I couldn't help being impressed.

"You could have chased her off."

"How? Then everyone would know about us."

"They already know. Crutch announced it at the Outhouse tonight."

"I heard about that," he said. "That's why I sent Crip to go get her to talk about it."

"You sent him to my house?"

"He wasn't there?" Strom acted surprised. I felt a chill and wondered if Alex was right. That Crip might very possibly be dead. Or that Strom was full of it, as usual.

"He was there." I checked for signs of disbelief. "But he didn't stay long, and I don't know where he went afterward."

"Did he take Sally with him?"

"They fought about it, but then she went."

"You didn't try to stop him?"

"He said you sent him."

"Good girl." He leaned over my lap and punched four numbers on the phone on the night table. "Lars, get over to Crip's place. Pick her up. And have Smith guard the entrance here. I don't want to be bothered." He put the phone down but didn't get off my legs.

"Lars told you I was here." He nodded and nibbled my fishnetted thigh. I felt like the catch of the day. "Strom, wait," I said, but he didn't. I found myself easing back onto the bed with his weight on top of me. Albeit, this was my plan A for the early hours, but it was, and always is, my prerogative to change to plan B. I said, "I'm keeping my partner."

"Are you still in love with him?"

"How do you know about that?" He stopped grazing on my neck for a second and then resumed.

"Crip told me," he said. "Keep him if you want him." Strom's gentle caresses turned more aggressive, and I recalled what Crutch said earlier about what would make me come. I put my mouth on his shoulder and bit as hard as I could.

"What the fuck?" he asked. "That hurt."

"When you hooked up with Crutch—Sally—you were sixteen."

"Around then."

"You told me your mother died when you were ten."

"What of it?"

"You said you fell for Crutch to get over your mother. Six years later? Not to imply it wasn't devastating, but you must have figured out a way to deal with it by then."

"You're underestimating my sensitivity."

"Or maybe you're trying to hide something." His eyes churned darkly. He seemed angry, but with Strom it was hard to tell. "Do you remember Flush wearing a gold locket on a chain?"

"Forget about Flush. I hired you to get the money, and we don't have much time."

"I'm closing in, don't worry about that. But the locket—do you remember it?"

"I think so. Yeah, a gold locket. It was round."

"My colleague discovered it and there was a picture inside."

"You mean Beaudine? Where'd he get it?"

"From Flush."

"Yeah? You think he and Flush were working together?"

"On what?"

"What do you think?"

"They fooled around."

"Then I guess that's what they did." I looked at him, puzzled. He said, "I don't give a shit about this locket if it doesn't get my money back."

"Yeah, yeah. But what did Alex and Flush work on together?"

He ignored my question and brushed his hands over my breasts. "Anyone ever told you you've got tits to write home about?"

"That's a funny thing for you to say."

"They're a nice set."

"I mean for someone who doesn't have a home."

"It's just an expression." He drew my arms over my head and held firmly to my wrists. "No more business tonight," he instructed.

"Who lives in this room?"

"No one."

"Who used to?"

"The accountant for Bisque-Mark, Inc. I had to kick him out when we went under. He's nobody."

"He left his clothes."

"I'll mail them tomorrow," he said and unlaced my bustier. My set sprang free. If Strom didn't like to use his mouth to speak, he compensated well in other ways. A groan escaped from my lips and I struggled to restrain myself.

"So who was spying on us at dinner? And when I came here the first time."

Strom cupped one hand under my chin and squeezed my jaw. He said, "You're not in charge when you're alone with me."

"Does this accountant have a key?"

"Do you think you can be polite and shut the fuck up?"

"I know you don't love me for my ladylike refinement, so politeness is out of the question."

He flipped me on my stomach. My wrists were bound by his grip. He pushed my skirt up around my waist and tore off my fishnets. He didn't bother with my underwear, he just pushed them aside, allowing only enough room for access. I heard the sound of a zipper, so I knew what was coming, but he entered me so suddenly that my breath caught. I tried to say something, and he pushed my head into the lace-covered pillow. I could barely breathe and move not at all. I was thinking how much I hated it, that is, until I came. If my mouth hadn't been muffled, I would have screamed. Strom came soon after and rolled over on the bed, freeing me. I gasped for air and bolted upright.

Before I could say anything, he stated, "Don't tell me I'm a liar again, Wanda. I think we both know now what the truth is."

I had no idea what he meant by that. I think he was trying to explain that he knew me better than I knew myself or something as deep as a wading pool like that. However well he thought he understood what I wanted, I remained in the dark about him. I wondered how one person could feel so entitled. And I wondered if everyone who worked for him hated him and loved him intensely and equally. But most of all, as I sat shivering next to him in our underground lair, I wondered if I should get back into therapy.

CHAPTER EIGHT

Rip This Joint

The first thing I did after I got the hell out of the Blood & Iron Headquarters at ten-ish was call Alex from the street to make sure Crip Beluga hadn't shown up during the night and squired Crutch away to suffer atrocities unknown. Alex reported that he hadn't. Nonetheless, I didn't feel safe with them staying in my apartment. The morning was young. Lars and a pack of biker mongrels might still show. I told Alex to take Crutch to Savarin, a Greek coffee shop on Flatbush Avenue, and not to leave or let her go until he heard from me. He was surprisingly amicable, considering the way I'd treated him the night before. Part of me regretted our spat, but I couldn't very well apologize for nighttime thinking, or take back things that couldn't be unsaid. I resolved to deny it. I flew like a bullet to the Do It Right office.

Times Square was bustling as usual with Caribbean incense sellers, dealers, beggars, thieves and the lonely Jehovah's Witness screaming through an amp to convert damned sinners. I walked up the four flights and found the office door locked. A good sign. The

TDK neon strobe on the Newsday Building winked at me as I stripped. I'd been wearing my heels and mini for too many hours in a row and my waistline was killing me. I keep a pair of 501s in my bottom desk drawer. There's also a Benetton cardigan (black), a pair of Vans (red, no laces) and a bottle of Love's Baby Soft Rain Scent (green). I changed and perfumed and felt somewhat more relaxed. My headache diminished not at all. I was hung like a pony. It could have been worse. I reminded myself that sleep deprivation could be spiritually enlightening. For no good reason—which is often the best reason possible—I helped myself to a few snorts of Amaretto. Not exactly hair of the Mescal worm, but it helped. I was ready for the day and whatever news it might thrust down my throat. I checked the messages—none. And I spent some time flipping matchbooks into a hat. I lit my first cigarette of the day. It tasted swell.

A call came in around noon. By then, I'd missed about fifty tosses and lit a half-dozen cigarettes. It was from Detective Dick O'Flanehey from Beekman Downtown Hospital. The emergency room. My immediate reaction was fear for Alex. Instinctive protection. I knew he was safely drowning in a plate of poached eggs on toast and home fries, extra grease—his usual.

"Cupcake," Detective Dick barked into the phone, "you are in all kinds of trouble."

"Tell me something I don't know."

"Get your ass down here. That's an order."

"Who shall I say sent me?"

"I'll be in Admitting." He hung up. I dreaded going back out. It was no more than fifteen degrees and I didn't have socks (or underwear, for that matter). I trudged out into the crispness and hailed a cab on

Broadway going downtown. I checked for Nick Vespucci in his gray limo behind me, but I saw nothing. I settled into the leather back seat and unpeeled my pinky splint. Three days should have been enough healing time, I figured. And I'd had it up to there with dainty hand gestures.

Dick was waiting, just like he promised, with a scowl under his mustache. Detective Tom "Bucky" Squirrely was nowhere in sight. I smiled when I saw Dick and said, "What, no flowers?"

"Our star witness took a few blows last night. We found him in Tompkins Square Park under a pile of garbage with his legs broken." Tompkins Square was practically a commune for bum junkies, in all kinds of weather. A year or so ago, the homeless residents staged a riot that ended with five dead—and none of them were cops. Legend has it you can't help smelling phantom blood and the stench of sizzling Molotov cocktails when walking anywhere near the borders. I've never noticed it, but then again, I've never walked through the park. There are places in Manhattan that spook even me.

Dick cleared his throat. I said, "You said *he* got his legs broken. Is it safe to assume, then, that your witness is a man?"

"Cut the crap, cupcake. I don't have killing time today."

"What room?"

"346. He whined off all the nurses."

"That Crip," I sighed, "you can't take him anywhere." Dick raised his eyebrows at me. "What," I asked, "you don't think I do my homework?"

"Lucky guess."

"Luck's got nothing to do with it, flatfoot." I half-lied.

155

Dick grimaced and found a smushed Twinkie in his back pocket. He unwrapped the plastic and sucked out the creamy innards. A drop of Amaretto rose up in my throat and it didn't taste sweet. Dick had white gunk on his chin when he said, "He won't talk to us. I told him to fuck himself, he's going downtown, if he doesn't."

"You can't get much farther downtown." Beekman is on the Manhattan side of the Brooklyn Bridge right by City Hall. Smith Jones and I almost flew over it when he whisked me home after my first night with Strom. My cheeks flushed with the memory and I coughed wildly to disguise it. "Nothing," I said. "This clean hospital air is destroying my lungs."

"Choke your guts up, I don't give a shit. As long as you get that moron Beluga to tell us who roughed him up."

"Are you asking me?"

"You want to know, don't you?"

"But you'd rather shit bricks than let me in there."

"I've got no choice," he lamented. "Beluga asked for you."

I smiled smugly. "Well, then," I said, "this is a bargaining chip of a lifetime, don't you think? Tell you what. We trade. Make a deal."

"No dice, sweetheart. I don't cut carpet with no girlie shamus."

"Spare me the colorful language, Dick. I want information on Flush Royale, and I want it now."

"Nothing to give."

"Bull dink."

"Badge carriers don't lie."

"Double bull dink." I turned and pretended to walk away.

"What do you want from me?" he asked impolitely.

"The locket."

He narrowed his eyes, trying to figure out what I knew. I raised my snottiest poker face and smirked. He said, "We don't have it."

"Who does?"

"You're killing me, Mallory."

I wanted to see him squirm. "I've got a lunch date."

"We gave it to Beluga to scout around, and he let someone take it away from him."

"Whoever snapped his femurs."

"Could be. Now, let's go. Put this in your pocket." He shoved a voice-activated micro-recorder in my hand. It bumped my pinky, and the pain made me wonder if I'd taken the splint off prematurely.

"Not so fast, blue boy," I said. "I haven't heard jack about Flush."

"One hint, and that's it."

"Two, damnit." He snarled like a hound dog from hell. I relented, "One hint is good."

"We followed up a missing person's report on a nurse's aide at the Lemon Tree Convalescent Home in Forest Hills," Dick said. "The dead kid matched the description."

"And she's the one?"

He nodded like he hated it. He said, "These needle jockeys are pumping Beluga with morphine in twenty minutes. We go now."

"How is he?"

"Doc says he'll never walk straight again." Cruel fate, that. It was as if the bowlegged curse was waiting his whole life to come true. "Down the hall, first door on the right. Don't fuck this up, or I'll string you to the back of my cruiser."

"Aye, aye, skipper." And we went.

One uniform was planted in the hallway, and one

guarded the door. Dick and I sailed past him into room 346. It had pink walls and two windows, but from where I was standing, Crip's legs in traction obscured an otherwise pleasant view. A meal tray was propped in front of him—turkey with stuffing—and he seemed to be in absurd amounts of pain. Detective Squirrely sat on the cot next to the bed. He was picking his fingernails with a paper clip. Dick pushed me farther into the room, and I couldn't help feeling depressed. I hate hospital rooms, especially ones with no reminders of the FTD man. Crip slowly turned his head in my direction. Patches under his eyes were purple, his nose had reinflated and the red splotch on his jaw remained from Alex's wheelhouse. He uttered, "Dang-blast it. I want to talk to her alone."

"That's your cue," I said to Dick.

Bucky said, "I don't trust her one bit."

"You don't have to like it, Bucky," I said. "Just lump it."

"All right, children," said Dick. "Let's get this over with." He waved at Bucky and they left the room. Crip flapped his lips, one of which was split open, and I gestured for him to shut up. I took the recorder out of my pocket and popped the cassette. I unspooled the tape a few inches and sat in the cot Bucky'd just vacated. The hospital smell smacked me across the face.

"When's the last time you had a sponge bath?" I asked.

"My life has been hell in a bucket since you showed up," Crip whined. "No wonder Beaudine ran off on you."

"I didn't come in here for dating advice," I warned. "Say what you have to say, and I'll leave you in peace with your agony. And stick to the case, or I'll rap you upside the thigh cast."

"Dag-nabbit, woman."

"A hospital bed is not the catbird seat, Crip. It would make Detective Dick's day to ship you to the hoosegow, and he will, with one word from me."

"He can't send me to prison if I didn't do anything."

"Don't be an idiot—of course he can."

"Get this grub away from me," he moaned, making a feeble attempt to shove the tray away. "I think I'm gonna be sick."

"How did Smith Jones get Flush's locket?" At the sound of the name, Crip cringed as much as the leg weights would allow.

"Strom didn't sic him on me. He came by his lonesome."

"How do you know?"

"He told me."

"And risk Strom's wrath?" I asked. "I don't believe it."

"He left me for dead." Crip flitted his lashes, and I couldn't help feeling sorry for him. "Darlin'," he asked, "my Texas pie is itching like crazy. Scratch it for me?" My sympathy ended.

"From the top," I instructed. "Go slow if you have to. You called Strom when Crutch and I left."

"He was snorting like a bronc about what happened. He didn't want anyone to know about her. I told him I couldn't control her, but he was hopping mad just the same. He came right over to the Outhouse and sent me to go get her at your apartment."

"But you went to the Lower East Side. That's not Brooklyn."

"I wasn't going to Brooklyn. I was getting out. I'd been trying for a while. The cops said they'd help me, so I helped them. I knew Strom was going to kill Crutch when he found her—or have Lars do it—and that was the last straw. She's kin, after all."

"Big of you."

"Don't get rily, darlin'. I did the right thing. And I would have gotten out plum fine if Jones didn't hunt me down."

"He was tailing for Strom."

"No, dang-blast it. I already told you he was on his own. He tackled me in the park. He had a crowbar. My lip went first, then he pounded my legs, just above the knee. I'm on Demerol, but it hurts just as bad." He moaned to prove it. I tried to picture cute, ponytailed Smith Jones striking Crip with enough force to do that kind of damage. Crip continued, "Jones said he had to kill me. That I heard him make the call. I had no idea what he was talking about until I came to this morning. Then I remembered. It was last night. I left the Outhouse on my way to my apartment to pack, and I saw him on a pay phone on East 7th Street. I didn't think a thing of it—I see B&I bikers all over the East Village every day. I smiled at him real pretty when we made eye contact because I didn't want him to get suspicious. If he told Strom I was trying to get out, Strom would come after me himself, and I'd be dead for sure."

"I find all this random murder and pillage stuff hard to believe."

"They'd do it. Every dang-blast one of them. They have before and they will again. I just didn't want it to be me this time."

"So Smith saw you smile at him."

"And before I knew it, he was chasing me around

the pass into the park with that crowbar in his hand. I have no idea who he was talking to. What I do know is that if Jones or Strom or Lars hears I'm alive, they'll come and kill me sure as weed tumbles."

"Why aren't you telling this to the cops?"

"For one, they'll use me to draw Strom out. For another, I need you to do something for me."

"Forget it."

"I just fed you enough information to gain twenty pounds, and you won't do one thing for me?"

"If it means protecting you, I can't do it."

"Protect Crutch."

"Is this more cousinly love?"

"I do love her."

"Yeah, I remember. You love all women."

"She's holding something for me, and I need it when I get out. If Strom finds her, I'm finished." The money, I thought immediately. So Crip was the thief after all. No wonder he couldn't tell the cops. Alex was sure to be disgustingly cocky about this. I hated it when he was right.

I said, "This request puts me in a weird spot, Crip."

"What weird?"

"Strom hired me to find the money. And when I do get my hands on it, I'll pocket a hunk for my trouble."

"What money? The stolen money? Is that what you think?"

"You and Crutch worked together. It makes perfect sense. You wanted out, she wanted to ruin Strom. If he went under, you'd be free, and she'd get satisfaction."

"I wish I did have it, but I don't. And she doesn't, either."

"So what does she have that you can't live without?"

"It's personal."

"Then, by all means, do tell."

"It's none of your dang-blast business. Keep Crutch safe, is all I ask."

"I'll turn her over in a second if you don't tell me what she's got."

"I can't."

"Then, I'll assume it's the money and send Strom over to chat with you about it."

Crip would have tried to hit me, I'm sure, if he weren't hog-tied to the bed. He sucked his bottom lip. Finally, he said, "It's my novel."

"Get real, Crip."

"I've been working on it for five years."

"About a motorcycle gang."

"It's a coming-of-age romance set in the Wild West."

"Sounds promising." I lied.

"I've got some great characters. There's Swing, he's the young ranch hand who's in love with Catastrophe Kate. Based on Calamity Jane? You see how that works? There's the evil landowner, Mr. Sneed. And he wants Kate for himself."

"I smell movie deal."

"I've got my fingers crossed."

"But not those legs." He didn't laugh. "Look, Crip. I'll do what I can. And that's all I ever do." I put the cassette back in the recorder and fast-forwarded. Through the clear plastic front piece, I could see the tape mangle and twist around the spokes. I said, "I'll have the public dicks keep a watch on you."

"Much obliged, ma'am," he said.

"One more thing. If you didn't take the money, and Crutch didn't take it, who did?"

"The way I see it?"

No, the way Superman does. "Yes," I said.

"If Flush was killed in a squabble over the money, then the thief and murderer would have to be her partner."

"And who would that be?"

"Ask your friend Beaudine. He might have something to say about that." Just as he finished, a bored nurse came in with a large needle. I took the opportunity to escape.

Dick was waiting inches from the door. He darted at me and grabbed my arm above the elbow. He usually didn't touch, just threatened, so I was taken aback. I said, "I don't dance."

He said, "Where's the tape?" I gave him the recorder. He pressed rewind and the thing spit up like a baby. He raved, "What the fuck?"

I gasped, "Will you look at that? And the taxpayers of this city shell out through their ears to keep you working. Maybe you should cut down on the doughnuts and buy some decent equipment."

Dick's brown eyes bulged. He demanded, "Spill now, or you can kiss your P.I. license goodbye." A legitimate threat, I reasoned.

"All he said was that he thinks his life is in danger. He passed out after that, and I spent the next ten minutes trying to rattle him alive."

"I heard voices." That was Bucky.

"I was yelling at him to come around," I said. "Look, guys, he's fair game now. He had his shot with me and he blew it. Do whatever you need to do."

"Who the fuck are you to tell us how to run this investigation?" Dick raved further. "You're a two-bit divorce chaser. You don't know shit."

"Then, I'll be off. A pleasure, as always." And I

darted, leaving the public dicks holding theirs as old ladies in wheelchairs entrapped them at the nurses station by forming the post-lunch double line for medication. Once outside, I lit a cigarette and decided what to do next. I wasn't so sure Crutch wasn't the thief, and for that matter, the killer. And I needed to devise a plan with Alex to find out who Smith Jones really was, and to whom he could have been talking on the phone last night. I hopped the 4 train at City Hall and headed into Brooklyn.

She was there—the pickpocket sat alone in an empty front car, her head resting on the subway map behind her. Her coat was open, revealing a Friday-night-date dress, black Norma Kamali knock-off, and tacky, shiny heels. Her bouf added five good inches to her head and her makeup was smeared from kissing. There was nothing quite as embarrassing than returning home on a Saturday afternoon, knowing that anyone who wanted to could guess what you had been doing the night before. And they'd guess right. She seemed tired, maybe too exhausted to hit a mark. Then *he* came in. She perked up noticeably and so did I. This was subway voyeurism at its best.

He was an older man—maybe forty-five, in a Members Only leather jacket with a full head of gray hair. There was nothing about him I found attractive, but he seemed to have money. He sat across from her and closed his eyes. We three were the only people in the car. If she was going home, she'd exit at the Grand Army Plaza stop, one after Bergen Street on the IRT. I eyeballed her as she sized up the situation. Members Only was sitting, the car was empty, a witness (me) was present. It'd be a challenge, and she seemed to know it. As we neared our destination and she'd done nothing, I figured the operation was a bust. But at Atlantic Avenue, one stop before ours, she spun into action.

The heels were a perfect prop. She rose to her feet and pretended to read the advertisement above his head about a free hemorrhoid exam from Dr. Tusch. The train lurched as if on cue, and she fell across his lap. He was startled, and upon finding an attractive woman squirming around on his groin, he smiled and placed his hands on her waist to steady her. She righted herself and then climbed to her feet, right as the train pulled into Grand Army. I couldn't spot the swipe. She smiled embarrassedly at the gentleman, and he ate it all up. Then she and I stepped off the train, free and clear.

A light bulb flashed somewhere, and I cozied up beside her as we hit the platform. I said, "Wait up." She turned to look at me and elbowed me in the ribs. Then she ran. I caught her just inside the turnstiles and pinned her against the staircase leading to street level. I reached into my bag, pulled out Mama, and buried the gun barrel under her chin. I said, "Hi. I'm Wanda. I like your style."

She spoke Brooklynese. "Yeah? I hate yours." I reached into her coat pocket and withdrew the hot wallet. I placed it in my bag. "Hey, that's mine, you bitch," she squeaked.

"Most people with a gun to their head don't call the person holding the gun a bitch. Let that be your first lesson."

"Yeah? Well fuck off." I couldn't help laughing at how gutsy she was. She seemed to have no fear at all.

I said, "I'm a private investigator and I want you to work for me. One job, and you get the wallet back."

"I'm not doing nothing for you except telling you to fuck off." She had the kind of spunk you generally find in pit bulls. I liked her.

I pressed the barrel deeper into her flesh. Concern flashed across her eyes for a second, then disappeared. I said, "I won't take no for an answer."

She said, "OK, I'll do it." I released her. She kicked me in the shin. I ignored the pain and got her against the wall again. This time, I stuck the gun in her belly.

"There's a police station three blocks from here," I said, rubbing my shin with my Van. "It'd be no trouble for me to haul you down there. We can look at the pickpocket complaint docket with your description all over it. And I bet the cops would love to join the party." She growled. I said, "Your choice—me or the cops."

She said, "Fuck off."

"Conversation is much more useful with a broad vocabulary. Let that be your second lesson."

"What do I have to do?"

"Nothing you haven't done before."

"I'm not stealing nothing."

"You steal all the time."

"Fuck you. You don't know what I do."

"This fuck thing. It has to stop."

"Yeah? Well fuck off."

"I've seen you steal wallets from three different men."

"I return them."

"Contents full?"

"Yeah."

"I don't get it."

"Yeah, well, you don't have to."

"I'm going to lower my gun now," I said, "and you

and I are going to get some lunch. I'm buying, so don't say you can't afford it. Give me your bag."

"No fucking way." I took it, found her wallet inside, and shoved it down my pants.

"You'll get it back after lunch. Don't make that face. There's a cute boy where we're going." That seemed to soften her considerably. She turned and stalked up the stairs. Grand Army Plaza has a marble fountain with a bust of Kennedy implanted on the front. Prospect Park sprawls just beyond the arch at the plaza. The same architect designed Central Park years earlier, and he said he righted all his mistakes with the Brooklyn landscaping. During the summer and spring, the flowers and Botanical Gardens are pretty enough to make you weep. I don't get to the park much. When I do, it's to take romantic strolls through pseudo-nature. The pickpocket stayed a step in front of me on Flatbush. She had a sleek walk. I made a mental note to buy some running shoes.

We got to Savarin, and I was starved. Alex was on the pay phone by the door. He saw me and said, "I was just calling the office."

"Alex, this is . . . what's your name?"

She smiled at Alex in his six-foot glory and said, "Lola Lizanski, pleased to meet you." She held out her hand and Alex shook it. He seemed bemused.

"She's the clumsiest pickpocket I've ever seen, and the best. She's going to help us with the case, right, Lola?" She nodded, but I didn't think she heard me. She was staring at Alex's collarbone. "Where's Crutch?" I asked.

He was grinning at Lola, when he said "Back booth." I couldn't tell if he was interested or not—she was definitely in his age range. He seemed to be revving up to full-charm throttle, but then again, Alex can't take a shit without flirting with the toilet paper. I strode into the diner to find Crutch.

She was smoking with her good hand in a vinyl booth, drinking coffee and wearing my cropped purple J. Crew sweater and my French Connection navy leggings with her heels. The overall look was horrid. I didn't care about the sweater, but the leggings were in obvious strain from her behind. I said, "Morning."

She said, "Afternoon, and I've got things to do. This kid Alex is cute, but not enough to keep me here much longer." She rested her head on the sticky wood paneling like she couldn't take any more.

"Strom heard about our tiny altercation, and he's no happy camper. If you go anywhere in Blood & Iron territory, he'll kill you or have someone do it for him. Maybe all those errands aren't so pressing now, huh?"

She giggled like last night. I wondered if she'd taken another Valium. She said, "Did he screw you? Did he hold you down and take you by surprise? Did you come?"

I would have answered, but Alex and Lola were approaching. They slid into the booth, Alex next to Crutch, Lola next to me, and my regular waitress, arthritic Mrs. Kiney, came over for my order. She said, "Miss New York," (that's what she called me—long story), "what'll you have?"

I said, "Two over medium, rye toast, coffee. Lola?"

Lola batted her lashes (they were purple, by the way) and asked with more than a little saccharine, "May I please see a menu?" I wondered if she always changed so much in the presence of an attractive man.

With a shaky hand, Mrs. Kiney gave her a menu, and Lola ordered a fruit salad with cottage cheese. She said to Alex, "I have to be careful for my figure." I wondered what she'd have ordered if it had been just us girls.

Alex smiled with teeth and said, "Don't be too careful. You might ruin perfection." My stomach lurched.

"Save the mush for breakfast, Alex." That was me. "Crip Beluga is harnessed to a hospital bed in Manhattan. Both his legs are broken. I made a promise I'd keep Crutch—Sally—out of trouble, and I mean to keep it."

"Is he OK?" That was Crutch.

"He's grousing about his novel."

"He told you about that?"

"Where is it?"

"My place."

"Alex," I said, "go get it. Crutch can't go with you—I guess she should stay out of Manhattan. Lars probably has her apartment staked out."

"What about you?" That was Alex.

"Lola and I have some sleuthing to do in town."

The food came and I wolfed mine down. Lola took little bird nibbles, and I felt like a pig. I got up to make a call and told Alex to come with me. We got to the pay phone in front, and I picked up the receiver. I dialed, but put no money in the slot.

Alex watched and said, "What's up?"

"Pretend I'm on the phone."

"Is this about Crutch?"

"This is about you, angel. Crip Beluga seems to be under the impression that you and Flush schemed to steal the money from the Outhouse safe, and in a fight over the division, you killed her and ran off with the *tout le loot*. Comments? Questions?"

"What does *tout* mean?" He smiled.

"Charm doesn't work on me. Anymore, at least."

"The theory is ridiculous, Wanda. And so is Crip." I believed him.

"Smith Jones did the number on Crip without permission from Strom. What do you have on him?"

"Ruthless pothead. Young, but experienced. He's been with B&I for a couple years."

"Any connection to Flush?"

"I never saw them together."

"Can't imagine she'd two-time you, huh?"

"Lola seems like a nice girl."

"Don't even think about it, Beaudine. She's all mine all day, and then she's history."

"I'd ask if you think I drool for every woman alive, but I don't want to get into one of those conversations right now."

"Good, 'cause neither do I."

"Good."

"Copycat," I mocked. "Speaking of which, did you feed Otis?"

"Shit."

"Goddam it, Alex. Can't you do anything right?"

"Mrs. Kiney recognized me. She asked where I'd been."

"What'd you say?"

"I said she looked nice and that I liked her perfume."

Before I could respond, the roar of motorcycles drew my attention outside. Through the front windows, I watched three bikers with long stringy hair, full beards, and sunglasses cruise slowly down Flatbush on their hogs. They seemed to be looking around. Once they rode past Savarin, the B&I emblem of a demonic, leering bat on their jacket backs came as no surprise. Damn, I thought. I slammed the phone back into the receiver and ran back to Crutch and Lola. Alex followed.

The two women were busy acting as uninterested as possible in each other. "Crutch," I said calmly, "you are to nod your head yes to everything I say." She sipped coffee. "There is a subway station one block from here. The D train. You and Alex are to walk there slowly with your collars up. Get on the train and go to the Adrienne Argola salon on the Upper East Side. Alex knows where it is. You are to ask for Santina Epstein. You met her last night. Nice lady. Tell her Wanda sent you. Tell her she is to show you the waxing room. Tell her Wanda told you not to answer her questions. Ask for a few magazines and stay there. Understood?"

She held up her splinted finger and said, "I'm going where?"

"Alex, take her. And explain on the way why her life depends on it. I'll be at Do It Right." Crutch squinted at me. Alex lifted her by the arm and they left, Crutch tentatively resisting Alex's tug. If she wasn't scared, she was an idiot, in which case she'd be too stupid to let someone help her. I tried to think.

Lola squeaked, "Hey. What about me? I want my wallet back."

"Eat your curds and shut up." If Alex and Crutch got off okay, that solved one problem. More bikers rode by outside. If Smith was waiting at my apartment, which was a good bet, Lola could try to get his wallet right there. That would take care of another problem. I didn't think he would hurt me, but I was no longer so sure I was under Strom's protection.

Strom must have learned by now that I lied to him about Crip getting Crutch. And for all I knew, the minions were after me anyway. I reached for my camel hair Donna Karan and thrust it at Lola. I said, "Wear my coat." I put hers on. It was a long black trenchcoat. It was pilling, but it'd do—it matched my hair.

Lola squeaked, "I'm not finished," and pointed at her cup with a spoon.

I dumped her fruit salad in the ashtray. "You are now. Come on." I threw a twenty on the table. I didn't know if Alex had already paid for Crutch and himself. On the way out, I said to Mrs. Kiney, "Hold my receipt."

Unless Lars or Smith were waiting for me, the bikers would be looking for a brunette in a tan coat. Lola was blonde, so they wouldn't stop her. We rounded the corner to my block. At least ten B&I bikers were stationed outside my building. I couldn't decide if Strom would say I'd be wearing glasses. I wasn't when I left him that morning, so I put them on. I didn't spot anyone I recognized. We walked closer. I wondered how much I'd be pushing my luck to pretend I lived elsewhere in the same building. Lola clicked recklessly along in her heels. If she sensed any danger, she didn't show it.

Getting inside was a matter of life or death; Otis needed to be fed. All right, maybe she wouldn't die from one missed meal, but I wanted to know what the horde would say when I asked why they were on my stoop. The plan would blow if anyone made me. A high-risk gamble for sure—Santina would be so disappointed—but it was one I had to take. As we inched closer, the smell of leather and grease assaulted my nostrils. I put my hand on the back of Lola's back to propel her along. She said, "Get your fucking hand off me."

"Shut up, you idiot."

"Don't call me an idiot, asshole."

We were doors away from my building. The bikers stared like we were naked. I whispered to Lola, "I mean it, shut up."

"Butthead."

"Asswipe."

We arrived at my stoop. My legs were jump-steady. The bikers didn't say a word, to us or each other, as they checked us out. They'd clearly been clued as to what to look for. Thank God I had switched coats.

I was standing at the door, slipping the key into the lock, when one of the bikers grunted. I turned around. The noisemaker was a particularly hirsute gentleman on a Harley that rivalled Lars' in chrome overkill. I recognized him from Alex's photograph of Smith with his soldiers. "Which one of you is Wanda?" he demanded.

Lola looked at me and didn't open her mouth. I was wrong—she was no moron. I said, "Wanda who? Do you mean the Wanda who lives on the first floor?"

"Broken finger," he said. "Let's see your hands. Both of you."

We held out our hands like a Palmolive commercial. "Petal pink manicure. Like it?" I asked.

The big guy said, "No splint. Get going."

"What do you want Wanda for?" I asked. "Is she in trouble?"

The hairy animal de-straddled his hog. His legs looked like pipelines. He stomped up the stoop and the dozen other metal men cheered him. Even two steps below me, he was half a foot taller. He leaned into my face and said, "That ain't none of your business, is it?" His breath was ghastly.

I said, "Not my business, nope." And we slipped into the building. I told Lola to crouch down and crawl to the back. They'd see us from the front windows otherwise. I scampered on my hands and knees and fed Otis. She seemed happy—Liver Puree. Then I crawled in back and put on socks. I told Lola we had to go. She stood to walk out, and I had to tackle her. She took the hint, and we made it back out without being spotted through the front window.

I closed the outside door behind us and pivoted to lock it. My back to the horde, I couldn't help smiling to myself. A dozen massive men, waiting in the cold for the woman right in front of their noses. If I ever got Strom back on my good side, I'd have to tell him to find new help. I spun cockily toward the street. Someone was standing at the bottom of the stoop. The familiar ponytail registered immediately, and I could have sworn I saw a blood mark on his well-worn overalls. My arms shot up on instinct, as if to block the horrid vision, and I knocked Lola in the nose. She said, "Watch it, you jerk."

Smith Jones said, "Wanda, babe. Guess who's in the hospital?"

I shook my head like I didn't know. His red eyes sparkled with a mixture of pot and insanity. And I'd assumed it was all pot.

"Sick people," he said "Get it? Got you again." He threw back his head and laughed, heh, heh, and I noticed the locket was missing from his naked neck.

"That's a real knee-slapper, Smith." I forced a smile. "What brings you to sunny Park Slope?"

"I think you know where you're going, babe."

"Straight to hell, I'd assume."

"I don't know about that," he said. "But we sure ain't going to Disneyland."

CHAPTER NINE

Road Trip to Hell

Lola whined next to me at the top of the stoop. She arranged one ankle at a neat three-quarter angle and said, "What the fuck is this? You didn't say nothing about no scumbags."

"Lola," I said, "this is Smith. He's the friend I wanted you to meet." I attempted a wink and hoped she'd get the hint.

"This guy? Fuck that," she sneered and sized him up with her head cocked. "Look at him, will ya? He's dirty, smelly, greasy, and obviously broke. He's probably got some disease, for all I know." He was also pathologically homicidal, I thought, picturing Crip's mangled gams. The biker pack guffawed and harrumphed wildly at Lola's appraisal. One long-armed Harleyite smacked Smith, with camaraderie, between the shoulder blades.

"Shut the fuck up. All of you's." That was Lola. "It's a fucking mob of greaseballs."

To my relief, Smith seemed more embarrassed than insulted by any of this. At least the slimes gave rope to blonde women. I sized up the odds. Twelve-on-one seemed a mite partial, and I doubted that I could handle Smith by my lonesome, besides. I said, "Too many cooks spoil the goulash, Smith."

He asked, "What, these guys?"

"This is no good on the street," I said. "I have neighbors. With binoculars. It's tacky."

"No class," added Lola. "Fucking scumbag."

I winced. With that comment, I figured her rope was up and I expected Smith to perform an unanesthetized tracheotomy on her. Instead, he lowered his head and looked at his blackened fingernails. His ponytail sprung up in back. Lola was right that he was scum, but with a regular cleansing regimen, Smith could be a babe. He raised his head and glanced quickly at Lola. She smirked and faced heavenward, as if praying to be released from his gaze. Then, she eyeballed him, all glossy-like. I could have sworn I saw him blush, but it might have been from the January wind. Lola drew her arms around her back and held her hands together—the result, a sudden increase in bust girth. Smith noticed and lengthened an inch. Lola caught that and moved her shoulders to and fro. Smith looked at his nails, then back up at Lola. He grinned like a little boy who'd just found his long-lost Tonka fire engine.

It was love, all right. And it filled me with wonder and hope. This tiny drama was witnessed not only by me, the pack had picked up on it too. We all watched in silence. There was something magical about it— even the mongrels seemed touched. I briefly contemplated the sweet mysteries of life.

Smith hooked his thumbs under his overall straps and said forcefully, "LOGHEAD." The humongous pelted one *ja wohl*-ed to attention. "Take off. Tell Strom I'll be there in an hour. I'll have Wanda with me."

No sooner said than done, the swarm flew away, down Flatbush Avenue to the Manhattan Bridge. They sailed in pairs, colors flashing, motors roaring. It was quite a sight to behold, especially when they pulled up at red lights. I was glad I'd worn my glasses.

Smith aimed his peepers at Lola. As if drawn by his beams, she stepped toward him, swinging her bony hips like they were on pulleys. He fidgeted with her approach, fearful and excited by the bounty in store. I felt a well of mushy-gushy rise in my throat as they neared each other—better that than Amaretto. I wondered if this would qualify as a Kodak moment.

On the last step of the stoop, Lola's heel nicked a tiny patch of ice, and she stumbled forward in an unflattering posture. Smith scooped her up just as she was about to hit asphalt and slung her, Tarzan-style, in his arms. She smiled prettily and batted her purple lashes. She swished her arms around his neck. They remained still for a moment too long. Then he lowered her gently and purposefully to her feet. I marveled at how this tender man could have hammered Crip's legs into a meaty pulp with a rusty crowbar.

The image snapped me quickly out of my Vaseline-lensed love mode, and I felt a rush of protectiveness for Lola. I grabbed her wrist and pulled her away from him. "Let's go already," I said to Smith. "Lola has to be somewhere."

"We can drop her," he said.

"That'd be real nice," Lola chirped.

"She wants a ride," he confirmed.

"Then, take her home," I said. "I'll wait here." The implication was obvious. He knew the bike could take only two. Smith's internal struggle formed a tic-tac-toe grid on his forehead.

"You won't wait," he guessed.

"It's her or me, Einstein."

He turned to Lola. She smiled and said, "Will you call me?"

"I don't have your number."

"Wanda does," Lola said, and she focused on where her wallet was shoved down my pants.

Smith said, "There's this great Scottish restaurant we can go to."

"What's it called?"

"McDonald's," he said. "Heh. Heh."

She didn't like the rib nearly as much as he did. For chicks, date venues are no joking matter. She turned and air-kissed me good-bye. I had no idea why she was suddenly so touchy-feely. That is, until I felt the weight increase in my coat pocket by one wallet. As she pulled away, she said, "Thanks for showing me your place," which really meant, I know where you live. Then she puckered at Smith and bopped up the street in her heels. Damn, I thought. My Donna Karan looked better on her.

Smith watched her as she turned left on Seventh Avenue. He said, "Nice girl."

"Full of surprises."

"So what's her number?"

"I'll give it to you later."

"I don't think you'll be able to." His eyebrows straightened.

"Call the Super-Scrub Car Wash on Atlantic Avenue. Ask for Lola."

"She works there?" He seemed surprised.

"Sudses them up and hoses them down." A vein in his neck pulsed. That was clearly something he wanted to see.

"So you think I should stop by and say hello?" he asked.

"If nothing more, Smith angel, you'll get your pipes polished." He nodded, confirming my theory that love makes you stupid.

He spanked the leather seat and commanded, "On the bike."

I climbed up and thought furiously for an escape plan. Hopping off a chopper gracefully is an impossible feat, even at a stop sign. There're so many bars and spokes—and me, in my tightest jeans. Smith swung his leg around and slid on in front of me. He twisted the key, let out the clutch, and we varoomed off. He hadn't given me a helmet like the last time, and I feared for my noggin as we rumba-ed over potholes and shimmied between cars. I was brave enough to open my eyes only when we stopped for a red signal at the lip of the Manhattan Bridge.

A homeless man on the street rambled between cars, selling roses that glowed in the dark. It was still light out, so he could have been lying. He asked Smith if he wanted one for the lady and Smith didn't respond. He had his agenda—ushering me to my death—and that was all he'd allow himself to think about. The Roseman said I was a hot tamale and that Smith, the ugly goombah, should do whatever he could to keep me. I didn't know if I should have felt flattered. An empty taxi inched up beside us. I stared at the driver and she stared back. A silent agreement was made. Rosey babbled about my finger-licking-good lovin'. Smith's silence only egged him on. He had nothing better to do, so the daredevil beggar reached out and touched Smith's handle bars. The buffer zone was then broken. And so was Smith's concentration.

There was a flash of movement as Smith's forearm pounded Rosey across the ribs. I heard the sound of dry wood snapping under bare feet, and Rosey collapsed on the pavement in front of the hog. Smith cursed the unfortunate position and leaned forward to touch the man and see if he was alive, thus able to get the fuck out of our way. That gram of compassion was Smith's fatal mistake. With the reach, his hand slipped off the clutch and the motor machine stalled. I made my move. I flung myself off the bike and landed on the street. I heard Lola's coat rip. I scrabbled into the taxi next to us. The light turned green. My legs were barely clear, when my lady driver slammed the pedal, dusting Smith, stalled and trapped behind the body of the man he'd just clocked senseless. Car horns blared, and before Smith could jump-start up and maneuver the bike around Rosey (or mow over him), I was a speck in the maelstrom of vehicles desperate to reach Manhattan. But we weren't going that direction anyway. We'd exited pre-bridge and cruised safely along the Brooklyn-Queens Expressway. Next stop: Forest Hills.

If the escape was a gift from God, then He/She had an evil streak. I had only a five-spot on me, and still miles from the regal borough, the meter clicked in at ten smackeroos. I was wondering how I'd convince my savior cabbie to accept a check, when I remembered I was a veritable cornucopia of other people's money. I plopped the four wallets—mine, Lola's, Smith's, and the subway mark's—on the seat next to me. Before the all-important financial tabulation, I licked my chops and cracked my neck on both sides in anticipation. My voyeuristic impulses ignited like rum in a china bowl.

Lola's first. The wallet was red, with a Snoopy patch ironed on the front. It looked old and ratty, but it was well organized with credit cards (Visa, AmEx) on one side and video club memberships (Blockbuster, RKO) on the other. She didn't have a license, but hardly any native New Yorkers did. (Driver's education doesn't exist in high schools here, private or public.) On a baby-blue index card, she'd written "Today I Will . . ." A list followed: "Think positive thoughts, listen, smile, be interesting and interested." I wondered from what woman's magazine she'd copied that. On Hello-Kitty notepaper, she had a neatly printed list of men's names and their phone numbers with a description of their credit rating underneath each entry. This chick did not fool around. She'd exed out anyone with under a $2000 credit line on his Visa. As far as pictures went, she had a snapshot of a black cat playing with a toy mouse. It looked like Otis, only skinnier. A lot skinnier. I made a mental note to put Otis on a diet. Cash reserves: seven bucks, a shitload of pennies, and a token.

The mark's wallet was a snooze. Some frightening family pictures with a pair of fat twin kids. Boys. Mommy wore a sundress that highlighted her jiggly upper arms. She looked tired, annoyed, and mean. That ended my inspection—it was no fun rummaging through someone else's business if you felt sorry for him. Available resources: a traveler's check, unsigned, for twenty bucks and three singles.

Last, the wallet de resistance—Smith's. It was nothing more than a ratty black billfold with no pictures, no credit cards, no matchbooks from strip joints with babes' phone numbers written on the back in red lipstick. The cash count was nil, not even change. What I did find was two condoms (the wrappers looked worn), an AAA card and a driver's license. The description fit, as did the picture of Smith. His blond hair was down and straight, and he looked more like a bohemian Nazi than usual. I missed the name on the license until the second go-over. It read: Sonny Vespucci. I wondered if Strom knew.

The cabbie switched lanes and the swerve made me look up. In the next lane, a gray shark swam steadily along the highway. I dropped to the floor. On reflex, my pinky throbbed. I lifted my head to peek. There was no mistaking the black windows and the massive outline of balding Gigantor, tooling behind the wheel. Nick Vespucci, grandpappy from Sing-Sing, was, no doubt, his happy passenger. I couldn't believe I'd missed spotting them at the Bridge. And I'd been checking for Smith—I mean Sonny—for miles. Sonny could have called Saint Nick on his bike phone—but then again, he didn't have one. And even if he did, Smith probably assumed I was headed for sanctuary in Manhattan. No, something was amiss. I told the driver to ease behind the limo and follow it. She said, will do, and expertly rearranged the setup. Gigantor barely noticed the move. I wondered where we were going. I braided my hair and upped my collar. I sang Carpenters songs so I wouldn't get cocky. The surest way to change your luck is to think about it. So I stopped thinking.

We chugged into Forest Hills, former home of the U.S. Open before the tournament moved to cheaper digs in Flushing, next to Shea Stadium. I'd crooned my way through "Top of the World" and "We've Only Just Begun." The tunes fit the town. Downtown Forest Hills was as suburban as it got in New York City, with actual houses, front lawns, clean streets, young marrieds, and retired geriatrics. The only nightlife was Joe's Calzone Hut, and that closed at ten on Saturday nights. We rode past squat municipal buildings after hopping bingo parlors, and eventually the shark glided into the circular driveway of the Lemon Tree Convalescent Home. How convenient—I wouldn't have to stop for directions. My cabbie glided to a halt at the corner across the street. She flicked off the meter as I watched Gigantor squeeze himself out of the car and open the back door for Nick. He was wearing his usual silk jammies and clutched what appeared to be a sizable strip of beef jerky. They disappeared inside.

My driver faced me expectantly. She deserved a big tip, and she aimed to get it. The meter flashed twenty-three samolians. I casually removed a check from my wallet and asked for a pen. She snapped her gum and announced, "No checks."

"I'm a little short." My cash total was only fifteen bucks.

She said, "I rescue you and follow a wiseguy limo through fucking Queens and you tell me you're short."

"I'll mail you fifty. Trust me. I'm a woman, I won't dick you."

"The sisterly thing won't cut it with me."

"Is there a cash machine around here?"

"We're in fucking Queens."

"How about a traveler's check?"

"Let's see." I showed her the mark's check and she dismissed it with a cluck. "Your name ain't Charlie," she said, "but I dig those earrings."

They were my Ylang-Ylang hanging pearls. Alex gave them to me for our six-month anniversary. When I went snooping at the store in Herald Center, the salesgirl told me they cost $45. Cheap bastard, I thought. I'd spent $200 on that stinking leather jacket.

"No way, Josie. Sentimental value."

"You don't got much choice." She smiled. Her teeth were quite lovely, actually.

I unhooked my baubles and threw them at her. "Take the fucking earrings," I said. "I hope you choke on them." She fished for them between the pedals and I split the cab.

The sign on the heavy glass door at the Lemon Tree announced the visiting hours. I had about half an hour left and too much to do. I decided to forget about Flush Royale and the possibility that she dished mush there for the time being. Saint Nick was more alive, and if anything made sense, his presence would have something to do with Flush anyway.

Inside, old people and their smells floated intrusively around me. I'd never seen so many wool cardigans in my life—a requisite on the dress code, I gathered. Withered guys and dolls were propped in plush corduroy armchairs aimed at nothing in particular. Some faced the TV in the lobby, some the window outside. None seemed to care what they looked at, if they could see at all. Orderlies in white dragged mops, and cute nurses in candy-striped outfits and orthopedic shoes pushed carts with mashed potatoes and trays of Dixie cups. I thought of my fiftyish parents living in retirement splendor in sunny Miami. They'd never have to endure a place like this, and I was comforted by that. I wouldn't have wished this grand finale on Hitler and Eva Braun.

The blue-haired lady at the front desk looked like Nurse Ratched pruned with gamma rays. She asked me who I'd come to see, and I told her I was supposed to be meeting my grandfather. She asked for a name, and I said, Nick Vespucci. Her hardened countenance melted, and she giggled like a virgin debutante. She said, "Your grandfather is such a sweet man. You're a lucky little girl."

"Luck's got nothing to do with it."

"He comes every Saturday, like clockwork."

"So that's why he never answers the limo phone."

"He's got a big surprise for you."

"I just love surprises." I lied.

"Well, the lady in question is in the room at the end of the hall. Last door on the right. Don't be frightened. She's not as dotty as you think."

I thanked her and walked toward the end of the hall. Gigantor loitered outside the room, flipping matchbooks into a hat.

"More wrist, baldie," I suggested.

He smiled when he saw me. "The bitch with the pee shooter," he said. "You a glutton for punishment or what?"

"What." I pushed open the door before he could stop me. He didn't follow me in. Maybe I was expected after all.

Nick sat on a chair next to a Victrola. He dropped on a thick piece of vinyl and lowered the tone arm. The concerto was lunar and gutsy and it sounded familiar—a strange assumption, considering that I never listened to classical music. The old woman on the single bed writhed lasciviously when the music penetrated her decaying earlobes. She had the tiny bones of a gentile, and sometime before the Crusades, she was probably quite a dish. Nick watched her groove under the covers, and I wondered if he could still get it up. I searched his lap for life and saw nothing. The record skipped and he lifted the needle. The woman's body froze, and her face assumed the animation of a burnt-out Buick. When the music started again, she contorted greedily away, grinding against the pillow stoved between her legs.

I was rivetted by her. I'd seen her face before—in Flush's locket. There was a photo of a sixteen-year-old boy on her night table. He was holding a stick and a Spalding rubber ball. I'd seen that face before too.

Nick didn't look up until he'd swallowed some jerky. Then he said, "Well, well. Wanda, dear. What a pleasant surprise."

I said, "All yours."

"I'd like to introduce you to my fiancée." The door opened a crack and Gigantor peeked inside. The old lady screamed. Nick hissed, "Get out of here, you brainless mass." Gigantor ducked out. "She's frightened of him," Nick explained.

I said, "Must be the glare from his head."

"The glare. Heh, heh. Well, no. He's supposed to be intimidating. In these chaotic days, one needs protection."

"Why not use Sonny? He's a slugger with a crowbar and a lot better looking." Nick's eyes danced at me. "There's definitely a family resemblance. You have the same breezy sense of humor."

"Yes, well. Sonny is a good boy. My only grandson. Strom doesn't know, so if you like going to the bathroom with your pants down, you won't share that with him." I watched the old lady. She didn't react to the mention of Strom's name.

I said, "You mean Morris, don't you?" And with that, the old lady stopped cavorting and her eyes filled with thick liquid. "Morris Blechman of Forest Hills? A rebellious child. Something of a firebug." The woman howled.

"That's enough, Wanda," Nick said sternly. He

turned toward the woman and cupped her face in his trembling spotty hands. "Mother Blechman," he whispered, "I have to go outside for a minute. I'll be right back."

"Eh? Whaddaya, whaddaya," she mumbled. "Mo-Mo."

Nick stopped the Victrola, stood slowly, and led me out by the elbow. Gigantor was waiting bashfully for punishment, like a dog who'd just pissed on the carpet. Nick smacked him across the face and pointed his finger menacingly at Gigantor's nose. "Why I oughta . . ."

I tapped his shoulder. "No more bullshit, Nick." He lowered his hand and faced me. "I'm tired, hung, undernourished, and overeasy. I know the whole stinking poop," I bluffed, "and if you want your money back, you'd better come squeaky clean."

Nick laughed, and I found more evidence of the family resemblance. Smith had the same neck, albeit fleshier. "If you think I want the money back," Nick challenged, "then you are far from the stinking poop."

Busted again, I thought. My bluff technique needed work. "Let's make a deal," I suggested.

"Well, hmm. No, I don't think so. Forgive me."

"I've got fifteen bucks. If that isn't enough, I'll give you my socks—cashmere. Soft and fluffy."

"Socks I don't need."

"I've got fingers." I cracked the knuckles on my good hand. Gigantor twitched with temptation.

"Wanda, dear. Desperation does not become you."

"If you won't take my virtue, how about taking Strom off my hands?"

"Forgive me, dear. But no one can barter with Strom. And what makes you think I want him anyway?"

"You dogged me all over town for dirt on Strom. And I've got the broken pinky to prove it."

"Lie to me and I'll break the other one."

"Strom's my love slave, don't you know?"

"Make that a thumb."

"Ten minutes alone with me and he'll sing 'La Marseillaise' in a tutu, straddling the Empire State Building."

"You must be tight as a fist."

"And I give a decent blowjob."

"Hmm. Well, yes, that's certainly something." He gnawed his jerky and chewed. "Gigantor," he said finally, "I feel like sitting. Warm up the car." The balding giant trotted off.

"Going my way?" And I'd been wondering how I'd get back.

"You appreciate a love story, don't you, dear?" he asked. "I sense that about you. Full of hope and joy. I'm the same way—a hopeful romantic. Notice how I say hopeful, and not hope*less.*"

"I noticed."

"I'll meet you in the limo." He popped into Mother Blechman's room to bid her adieu. I made for the great outdoors. The limo was purring, and Gigantor leaned against it with one hand on the hood, like he was keeping it from driving away on its own. He didn't open the door for me. I got inside. The mini-bar was stocked to the gills, and I fixed myself a margarita with salt.

Nick climbed in soon after and we sailed toward Manhattan. I said, "We go to my office. Someone waiting for me there."

"I doubt that, dear," he said. "More likely Beaudine's at the Blood & Iron headquarters with a tire iron stuck up his ass." Nick's eyes glistened at the thought. He tore into jerky with his dental daggers. "You hungry?"

The cord of panic tightened around my throat. "Alex would never let himself get caught."

"Whatever you say, dear."

I reached for the limo phone.

Saint Nick said, "There's nothing you can do. It hurts to lose someone you love, doesn't it?" I dropped the receiver back into the cradle.

"I wouldn't know," said Saint Nick. "I've never been in love before. Sonny's grandmother, she meant nothing to me. I thought I was supposed to get married at the time, so I did. She died, of unnatural causes. These are violent times, they call for violent measures."

"This rationalization thing? Is it catching?"

"But at long last love," Nick swooned. "Doesn't Mother Blechman smell heavenly?" Like a mixture of institutional shampoo and Salisbury steak, I thought. "I met her when I was staying at the Lemon Tree, recovering from a small operation," Nick continued. "Digestive problems. My stomach can only take so much roughage. This was a year ago. My stay lasted a few months, but it was long enough for me to meet Mother Blechman and fall in love. Music, my dear, was the elixir, and the first time I saw her dance, my heart melted. Oh, I know she seems a bit slow at first, but the depth of that woman. She's been through so much."

"Like when Strom burned the house down."

"Strom did what?"

"He told me he burned his house down with his mother in it. I take it the light of your life is the grandmother."

"Strom's been spinning a few yarns, hasn't he? Well,

no, actually, dear, the woman I love is Strom's mother. She got sick when he was a teenager. First his father left, and then Strom ran away when the responsibility got too much. At that age, his disappearance was almost forgivable. But he never came back. Never even called on Mother's Day."

"Ouch."

"Mother snapped when he left, and the city's health services put her in the Lemon Tree. She's been living in that same room since then, and she barely even spoke before Angelina—Flush Royale to you."

"Mother's nurse."

"And her friend. They grew close, and Angelina was the one who introduced Mother to Il Divino—Corelli to you. And she joined us together in love. Poor dear. Angelina was like a daughter to Mother."

"And Smith—he was like a son?"

"Sonny," Nick corrected. "He never met her. He takes care of my business, not my romance."

"Bisque-Mark Blades."

"A ridiculous idea—ceramic switchblades? Was he crazy? But Strom was referred by my grandson, and I couldn't say no to family. It wasn't until later that I realized Mother Blechman's Morris and Strom Bismark were the same boy. Then I had the answer to my prayers."

"A castle in France?"

"Heh, heh. Well, no, dear. Mother Blechman wouldn't marry me without her son being at the wedding, but she didn't know where or who he was. I'd been trying to find him for months when I made the discovery. And by then, Strom was into me for a hundred grand. I asked him, politely, to come to the wedding. Gigantor was with me, of course. It didn't go well. Strom was shocked his mother was still alive.

And he refused to come out to Queens. He has a distorted idea of how important his image is. The leader of Blood & Iron shouldn't have a mother, much less have contact with her. Can you believe the selfishness of that boy? He should be spanked. That's when I hired Angelina."

"To spank him?"

"It pained me deeply when I heard what happened to her."

"I bet it pained her more."

"I hired her to steal the money from the Outhouse safe. Then Strom would have to attend the wedding."

"You lost me."

"We made a deal. Strom had two months left on his payment schedule. He'd given me only a few thousand at that point, so I told him we'd forget the rest of the money if he would come out to the Lemon Tree and give his mother away. He asked for the remaining months to try and make the payment. I'd already made a schedule, and I gave him what was left of it. We shook. I thought about having Gigantor pick him up and bring him to Queens in a box. But I wanted it nice for Mother. And Strom's nearly impenetrable, even with Sonny on my side.

"So I waited patiently for his time to run out," Nick explained. "I never thought he'd get the money together. Things weren't so good for him. They still aren't. That's why I was surprised when word came down from Sonny that Strom was nearly there. I don't know how he did it, but he'd gotten the money together. I set my plan in motion. Angelina was in already. That idiot Beluga hired her and fell for her on sight. She was supposed to weasel the safe combination out of him. Sonny was supposed to protect her."

"He didn't do a very good job."

"She was killed before she got the chance to turn the money over. Sonny warned me something would go wrong. He said her new life changed her. I was worried. Keeping Strom from having money certainly did not lessen my desire to have it—agreement or not."

"You wanted your cake and to make Strom eat it too."

"Well, hmm. Yes, actually. But Angelina, lovely child, got herself a partner inside. She hinted that she wanted more of a payoff than the salary I gave her. I said no, and she promised she wouldn't cross me. But she lied. And died—of unnatural causes." I spit up margarita, leaving me soggy and salty in the backseat with a killer.

Nick said, "Enjoy your drink, dear. I didn't murder that girl."

"You wouldn't tolerate that kind of violence."

"And neither did Sonny or Gigantor." Saint Nick gnawed jerky.

"The killer salami's got your name all over it."

"A little reminder to Strom that his time was up. Sending it doesn't mean I clobbered Angelina with it."

"So who did?"

"Her partner, dear."

"And who might that be?"

"Strom had an idea. He bought time with it. And now I have a feeling his idea was right, and he's closing in."

"But you'd like to get there first."

"Well, yes. And that, my dear, is where you come in." Nick pressed a tiny button next to the TV console. The lid of a secret compartment sprang open like a jack-in-the-box. Nick reached inside, and I

193

thought for a crazy second he'd whip out a bouquet of flowers. But no daisy I'd ever known had steel casing and a snub-nosed barrel. He pointed the Smith & Wesson .38 at my open mouth and said, "Her partner was Alex Beaudine, and I want him."

The white highway lines bleeped by, and I guessed we were doing eighty. For a boat, the limo could haul ass. If I jumped out I'd pulverize myself—not a good idea. "Careful with that, Nick," I warned. "You don't want to ruin your upholstery."

"You're the only one who can get Beaudine," Nick oozed. "Strom was counting on that from the beginning."

"It's not Alex," I stated. "You're wrong."

"I'm right."

"You're wrong. I'm sorry. I know it sucks. But you're wrong."

"Strom has an eyewitness, dear. The only reason Beaudine stayed alive is because Strom needed the money more than he needed him dead. But that's probably changed by now."

"And you want me to invade the B&I headquarters with my battering ram and whisk Alex off on my trusty steed?"

"Into my torturous arms, yes." Nick rubbed his gray chin with the gun. "You can do it, dear. Strom is your love slave. And Sonny will help. A revolution has been brewing at Blood & Iron for a while. And its time has come."

"Making room for Sonny at the top."

"He'll be a brilliant leader."

"What if Alex is dead and Strom already has the money?" I asked.

"Then take it away from him."

Through the black windows, I saw the lights at the

South Street Seaport. We were almost there, maybe ten minutes away from the headquarters. Alex would never let himself get caught. I reminded myself of this for the hundredth time in three seconds. The idea was absurd. Alex was a master at dangerous escapes. Strom didn't have a violent bone in his body. Lars was a gymnast for Ringling Brothers. And Sonny was a poodle trainer from Brazil.

"My rate is $1,000 an hour," I said. "Your hour started twenty-five minutes ago."

Saint Nick pressed the intercom button on the TV console. "Gigantor," he purred, "step on it."

CHAPTER TEN

Shamus Blues, Reprise

Nick Vespucci didn't want to be seen, so Gigantor dropped me at the corner of Tenth and First, one block from the headquarters. I trudged up the Avenue in the cold. The tear in Lola's coat supplied unwelcome ventilation. Nick promised to have an escape vehicle for my hasty retreat whether I could wrangle the money or not. Right, I thought, and Mary was a virgin. My safety was not an issue for him. What he wanted was Strom's downfall, his ill-gotten gains, and the hand of his fair maiden—not necessarily in that order. Nonetheless, I marched forward to meet my destiny. Or Strom, whichever came first.

I sensed I was being followed. I turned to look and saw a thousand faces, but none that I recognized. I dodged my way through the Village revelry, falling into the rhythm of the street, dodging left, leaning right, aiming straight for hell. Slush soaked my Vans. I thought about dashing into a bar for a shot of mescal. Or placing a collect call to Santina at the salon to say howdy. I thought a lot of stupid things on that one-block walk and abandoned them as quickly as they came. If Alex was damaged in any way, I'd never get over it.

I closed in on the B&I building. Smith/Sonny patrolled outside. I approached him recklessly, full of meaningless courage. He said, "You shouldn't have run off."

I asked, "Is Alex in there?"

"You shouldn't have lied to Strom, babe."

"Is that right, *Sonny?*" His blue eyes bugged. I said, "Whose side are you on, anyway?"

"I'm on my side," he hissed, as if there was any other place to be.

Before I could respond, the blood-red doors flew open. Lars's massive bulk crowded the opening. He said nothing—his presence was enough of a command.

One goon on each arm, I was led to the library. The only light in the room came from Strom's dancing cigarette. He was sitting behind the desk at the far end. The cherry glowed red with an inhale, then back to orange. A gust of smoke floated under my nostrils. "I feel most comfortable in the dark," he said.

"My ex-shrink might say you've got something to hide."

"Less and less, it seems. Thanks to you." My eyes adjusted slowly, but I was close enough to see him squash out the cigarette. I hesitated before looking at his face. When I did, I noticed a string of dots across his cheek. It was too dark to discern their color. Either he'd exploded a fountain pen, or cut someone's jugular. "Bring in Beaudine," he barked, and Lars dropped my arm and left the room.

"Strom, honey," I cooed. "I missed you today."

"You lied to me," he said, boy scout that he was.

"I'm not the only one," I said, feeling Sonny's grip tighten on my arm. "Betrayal is all around you."

"Shut up," he yelled. "Just shut up, you stupid bitch. These people are my slaves."

"Is that right, Smith?" I asked. "Are you Strom's slave?" Sonny didn't respond.

"Smith," barked Strom. "Answer her."

"I'm your slave, Strom," he said through clenched teeth.

"That didn't sound too convincing," I commented. Sonny's breathing quickened. Just a few more jabs and he'd be mine.

"Your opinion means nothing to me," said Strom. "I only hired you in the first place to find out where Beaudine hid the money. But now it's too late. I'll kill both of you in a second."

I heard a crash. Lars had brought Alex in and hurled him to the floor. Sonny nearly cut the circulation on my arm as I tried to yank free. Lars lifted Alex by the hair—his beautiful hair—and tugged him over to Strom's desk. Blood ran from his nose. It was swollen and broken. He smiled weakly when he saw me and my heart crumbled. I said, "Alex, honey, I'm sorry I snapped at you. I was under all kinds of pressure. I didn't mean it. And now this. Please don't hate me."

Alex rasped sweetly, "Wanda, there's nothing you could do that would make me hate you."

"Well I hate both of you," said Strom. "And if you don't tell me where that money is, Wanda is the first to die."

"I told you already. I didn't steal the money. And I don't care if your witness is the Pope. He's lying." Alex was so cute when he was angry.

Lars drew his arm under Alex's chin. He said, "Are you calling me a liar?"

"You?" I asked.

"I caught Beaudine and Flush in Crip's office," said Lars. "They were working on the safe."

"Bullshit." That was Alex.

"And Beaudine ran out before I could stop him."

Strom nodded greedily. I dared to make a point. "So why on earth would Alex keep hanging around the Outhouse if he knew you saw him?" I asked. "Excuse my stupid female opinion, Strom, but that sounds a bit too masochistic, even for Alex."

Lars tightened his grip around Alex's neck. He said, "Beaudine didn't see me. Only Flush."

"That's not what you said two seconds ago," I observed.

Alex asked, "What happened to Flush, Lars?"

"You ran out, you didn't see me." Lars looked imploringly at Strom. "He ran out. They were partners."

Even in the dark, I could see the tornado behind Strom's eyes churn. He opened the drawer of his desk and whipped out a black .44 magnum, and I don't mean champagne. Sonny freed my arm and reached behind his back. I dropped my hand into my bag and brushed steel.

Lars said, "Strom, I'm telling the truth." He must have flexed his arm, because Alex choked.

"Where's the money?" Strom asked Lars as he walked, gun forward, toward the entwined Lars and Alex. "Where's the fucking money?"

"Let me explain."

"I'll blow your fucking head off."

"It was Flush's idea. She made me."

Alex gurgled, "What happened to her?"

"He did it," Lars accused. "Strom did it. He sent me after you and when I got back to the Outhouse,

Flush was dead on the carpet. He wrote the message in blood with the salami to confuse people into thinking he didn't do it himself."

Strom sidled up to Lars and stuck the black barrel in his eye. "She died because she wouldn't talk," Strom warned. "I'd hate to see that happen to you."

"No, you wouldn't." That was me.

"Shut up," Strom ranted. "Shut the fuck up."

Lars leaned away from the gun, lifting Alex off his feet by the neck. Even in the stranglehold, Alex managed to kick Strom in the shin. He snarled like a beast and the gun exploded. Two bodies collapsed on the floor, one with a head.

"Drop the gun, Bismark, while you still can." That was Sonny. He had his own pistol pressed against Strom's sinewy neck. Strom dropped the gun. It crashed to the floor with the same empty finality as Lars's useless bulk.

Alex pried himself free and rolled across the carpet to where the gun lay. He aimed it at Strom's nuts. A significant gesture, I thought, one I could not ignore. I joined the party and pointed Mama at Strom's heart.

Sonny said, "We'll tell the cops Lars killed Flush over a squabble for the money."

"The hell we will." That was me.

"Strom will get his, babe, but right now we've got a wedding to catch." Strom turned, puzzled, to face his treacherous enforcer. "Come on, Morris," Sonny said. "The limo's waiting."

"What about the money?" I asked.

"I guess we'll never know. Gramps will do OK without it," Sonny assured me, and he started to leave with his captive.

"Wait." Sonny stopped, and I walked up to Strom. I

slapped him across the face, hard. "Payback, honey," I said. "And you can take that personally." Then Sonny led a defeated Strom out to the street. He'd never looked so sexless.

I dropped Mama back into my purse and dialed the cops on Strom's desk phone. Alex struggled to his feet. He found the switch and the sconces flooded the room with light. Lars was spilling like Niagara. I looked away in time to catch the shoes behind the drapes disappear into the wall.

I told the desk sergeant to send Detectives Dick O'Flanehey and Bucky Squirrely to the Blood & Iron headquarters. I didn't leave my name. I hung up the phone and wiped the receiver clean. I found a cigarette in my bag. I lit it with my gun lighter and inhaled deeply. It tasted swell.

Alex said, "Did you know?"

"Did I know what?"

"That I was here."

"Yeah. I knew."

"And that's why you came."

"Nick Vespucci waved a thousand dollars in my face."

"Bullshit. You came for me." He made his adorable gummy smile.

"Do I have to admit it?"

"I wouldn't want to put you out."

"Then I won't."

"So don't."

I made smoke rings. "I had to give my pearl earrings to a cab driver."

"What earrings?"

"The ones you gave me for our six-month anniversary."

"I never liked those anyway."

"Cheap bastard."

"Selfish bitch." We grinned at each other. A gush of love welled up in me for him, but it was different. More friendly. Less erotic. It felt easier.

He wiped the blood from his nose with his sleeve. "Promise me you'll never sleep with a guy like Strom again."

"I wish I could." I put out the cigarette and dropped the butt in my purse. What Dick didn't find wouldn't hurt me.

"So Wanda," Alex said, "you think we should stay together? Working for Do It Right."

"Do you?"

"I want to."

"Whatever you want, baby," I said. "It's yours."

"Say, I want *you*," he taunted.

"Then we might have a problem." He smiled and things suddenly felt normal. And the only bad thing that remained between us was Lars's gushing headless body.

Sonny Vespucci darted into the library. He had a stack of bills in his hand. "Nick says thanks," he relayed as he gave me the money. "Wipe off Strom's gun and get out of here."

"He would have shot me next," Alex said. "Thanks, man."

"There's only one way to thank me," Sonny said. "Just tell me this. What's the difference between light and hard?"

"What?"

"You can turn a light off. Heh, heh." He chuckled. "Got you again." And then he left us alone.

Alex wiped off the gun on his shirt and dropped it

on the floor. He said, "The cops'll be here any minute. Let's go."

"You don't want to leave without the money, do you?"

"What money?"

"What money. Are you a moron? Nick's money. One hundred thousand dollars worth."

"You know where it is?"

"Follow me." I drew back the drapes to reveal the hidden door. The lock had already been fixed from the previous night, so I blasted it off again with Mama. Alex and I ran down the corridor. The end door was locked. Alex kicked it open.

"What is this place?"

"This is the private quarters of Strom's secret weapon. His mathematical, financial genius. The guy who really ran the Blood & Iron show." I spoke loudly, so my man in hiding would hear. "Strom was on the brink of disaster. This wiz had just two months to get Nick's money together for him. He's a genius, and he did it. And Strom would have been saved if he didn't steal the money for himself first, probably to impress a woman."

"Pray, Sherlock, who is this masked man?"

"It didn't occur to me right away. Those inventory sheets in the closet. Every possible five-number combination. Whoever lived in this room cracked the combination and stole the money from the Outhouse safe. I knew he was an accountant already. The only problem was that I didn't know who he was."

"Nice blackboard," Alex said.

"What tipped me off was the music. Archangelo Corelli. Il Divino, as Nick called him. Flush's favorite composer. A man in lust picks things up, like a girl's taste in music. The statue in the closet is of the composer. I've been humming his concerto for days and never knew what it was."

"I told you what it was," reminded Alex. "The *Christmas Concerto*. In G minor." I ignored him.

"Then I heard it again today," I said, "and something clicked. I remembered the first time—when he was humming it at the Outhouse. He didn't have much to say, but he sure could hum." I gestured wildly to Alex to look under the bed. That was the one place I forgot to check the night before. I'd had a lot of things on my mind, and getting *under* a bed wasn't one of them.

Alex looked at me flinging my arms around and said, "What the fuck are you doing?" I mouthed and pointed furiously. He had to be there. I saw his feet under the drapes. And there was no other escape except through the library.

Finally, Alex got the idea. He bent over and rested his head on the floor. "Hi, Billy," he said. "Want to come out and play?" Alex tugged at a shirt collar that eventually became a whole man in a crumpled suit. He stammered silently.

His calculator rested impotent and out of reach on the night table. Alex handed it to him and said, "Don't be shy." Billy punched numbers and showed me the pocket machine. It read: hI.LESLIE (317537.14).

"My name's not Leslie, and I want to make a deal," I said. "You keep half and like it."

Billy considered this. He didn't seem terribly nervous. And he didn't hum a note. He punched more buttons. It read: hELL (7734).

"I take it, that's a yes," I said. "The cops'll be here any minute. Give. Now."

He straightened his suit and went in the walk-through closet. I followed him to make sure he wouldn't try anything funny. I was confused. I'd already searched the space and found no greenbacks. I expected him to uncover a cubbyhole or a dug-out panel. He reached into the inside breast pockets of those crummy old suits on wire hangers and yanked out stacks of hundred-dollar bills. I almost spit. So I forgot to search the suits. So I'm an idiot. Alex thanked Billy as I deposited our five stacks in my bag. The weight of the money, along with the four wallets, dug the strap into my shoulder. Alex offered to carry it. I lovingly told him to fuck off.

We turned to hightail. Billy touched my shoulder. I expected him to punch out a message, but he surprised me by speaking. "I was under the bed last night," he said. "I heard everything. It was worth the fifty grand." I didn't know if I should feel flattered.

By nightfall, Alex and I had split the booty at Do It Right. He asked what Billy meant about last night and I said forget it. He shrugged and pushed hair off his face. Even with the swollen nose, he was utterly adorable. Alex left with his half as soon as we finished. He had errands, he said. I felt a pang of jealousy and wondered how old his errand was. But I was a good girl and kept my mouth shut. I filed my stack under S for smackeroos. And just as I closed the cabinet drawer, the public dicks barged through the office door.

Dick O'Flanehey twirled his mustache. Bucky Squirrely attempted an air of menace. "I know you know where he is, so save us some time and yourself some damage," Dick said with forced calm.

"Alex just left. I think he had a date."

"Not the beanpole," Dick raved. "Strom Bismark. No one knows where the fuck he is."

"Well, he dumped me yesterday," I said. "You boys should have done your homework."

Dick bared his teeth, clawed the air, and growled at me. I cowered in terror. Bucky, spotting his big chance, broke in. "There's been a murder," he reported. "And Bismark is wanted on all counts."

"What? A murder?"

"Lars Horowitz bought it tonight." Horowitz? "He tried to eat a .44 Colt Magnum. His mother never told him you can't digest metal."

Dick snapped, "Don't talk to her, you moron."

Bucky defended, "What's she gonna do?"

"Gentlemen," I interrupted. "I'm upset enough about Strom already. And right on the heels of Alex. Can't a heartsick girl agonize in peace anymore?"

"Don't give me that," Dick said.

"Can't you see I'm hurting?" I asked.

"Hurting like a massage, cupcake."

"I'm very vulnerable right now."

"Where's the money?"

"What money?"

"What money? You moron. Nick Vespucci's money. A hundred thousand dollars worth," ranted Dick. I had déjà vu.

"Oh, that money. I guess the secret died with Lars." I paused. "How's Crip Beluga, by the way?"

"He's doing OK. A few more weeks on his back." That was Bucky.

"I told you not to talk to her," ordered Dick. "And you," he pointed at me, "don't think you're going anywhere."

"I never do," I promised. Dick yanked a Twinkie

from his pants pocket and tore the wrapper off with his teeth. Bucky scowled as threateningly as he could muster. I yawned. They split like cleavers. I spent some time flipping matchbooks into a hat. I never wear the hat. I'm not a hat person.

I got two wedding announcements that Wednesday. One said that Nicolaus Vespucci and Lila Blechman of the Forest Hills Blechmans were married on Monday. The service was at the Lemon Tree Convalescent Home. Those bastards, I thought. They didn't even invite me.

The second card announced the reaffirmation of wedding vows by Morris Blechman and his wife, Sally Rosenstein, of the Flushing Rosensteins. This magical event was inspired by the discovery of their expected baby. The mother hoped it would be a boy. The couple would be moving in with his mother and her husband as soon as they could buy a house large enough for the entire family.

Sonny Vespucci was right—Strom sure did get his. Sonny assumed Strom's throne almost immediately. He got himself a nice girlfriend by Thursday and he reopened the Outhouse by Friday.

Crip Beluga remained in the hospital for a full month, care of the New York City Police Department. He started a new novel—a coming-of-age romance set in a big city emergency room. I never saw Billy again, no matter how many times I roamed the East Village looking for a bottle and a babe, not necessarily in that order.

I must have dozed off. I woke to the sound of glass breaking, with my nose in the hat. I looked up. Lola

Lizanski, in my Donna Karan, crushed what remained of my office door window under her tacky heels. "Where's my fucking wallet?" she asked, snapping her gum.

I'm never fully alive before the first three cigarettes and the first two cups of ginger tea. That Sunday morning was different. I was kicking in no time. It may have had something to do with a solid sleep. Or it could have been Lola slapping my face. "Cut it out. Jeez," I said, groggily. "It's in my bag."

She pounced on my pocketbook like Otis on a cockroach. Actually, much faster than that. After she'd checked the contents, first for her own, and then, her subway mark's wallet, she said, "Shit."

"I didn't take anything," I said. "I would have if there was something good. But I didn't take anything."

"I fucking know that. It's this asshole. He's married."

"What, you only pick bachelor wallets?"

"You don't know what I do. Fuck off."

"There's another wallet in there you might want," I said. "The black billfold."

She plucked Sonny's strip of leather out of my bag. She opened it and looked at his driver's license picture. She smiled, snapped her gum, and said, "Thanks." She shrugged off my camel coat and let it fall to the floor. She grabbed her own off the coat rack and slipped it on. I crossed my fingers, but she noticed the tear. "What the fuck?" she asked. "You better fucking pay for this."

I found a cigarette on my desk, and lit it with my head tilted. Highly dramatic. I inhaled and said, "Tell me why you pick pockets."

"Fuck off," she said and slid the wallets into her purse.

"I'll give you five hundred dollars."

"Bullshit."

"Try me."

She stared at me, trying to figure out if I was full of it. She must have decided I wasn't when she said, "It's hard to meet guys in this city, you know?"

"I know." I dragged my body out of the chair and over to my file cabinet. I asked her to turn around—she did—and I peeled some crisp bills from one of my stacks. I counted them out into her palm.

"Six?" she asked.

"Buy yourself some new shoes," I said. "Now, get lost."

She shoved the cash down her bra, told me she'd see me around, and left. I stepped around the broken glass and walked down the hall to the bathroom to do my business. I didn't bother to look in the mirror—I knew what I'd see, and the thought frightened me. When I got back to the office, the phone was ringing.

I picked it up. "Mallory here."

"Wanda? Thank God you're all right. You didn't come home last night. I was so worried, I didn't let Shlomo sleep for a minute. I said to him, I said, 'Where is she? She's goddamn dead because of that disgusting job of hers.' And that woman, that Sally creature? I told you twenty-seven million times, I will not, cannot, give leg waxes for free. It's enough I do my own legs if I'm looking for trouble."

"Santina, I have to go."

"If you were in law school, I'd do your homework. But I'm not doing your friend's legs."

"I appreciate the support."

"Your hair—that I'll do. I'm waiting at the salon and I've got a spot in half an hour. Maybe you should walk uptown. The exercise will do you good. Those legs of yours."

I hung up. A strand of black hair dipped in front of my eyes. That I'd dyed myself for Strom sickened me. I tugged on my coat, and after a quick stop in the bathroom to brush my teeth, I taxied to Adrienne Argola. The cabbie didn't have change for a hundred. He accepted a check.

Santina fluttered at me like a fascist butterfly when I walked in. Her beehive bobbed. She wore red velour that day—a not-so-subtle reminder of my former hair color, or just bad taste? "Wanda," she shrieked, throwing her arms around me. "You're as gorgeous as ever." I looked like shit and she knew it. Something was amiss. There were no other customers in the salon. Of course, I thought. Sunday morning.

A thin man in jeans and a Patagonia jacket swiveled to face me in a barber chair. I hadn't noticed him before, although I couldn't figure how I'd missed. He was a babe. "Max," Santina cooed, "this is my beautiful downstairs neighbor."

He got up and came toward us. He was taller than I thought. Santina dipped over to kiss me. I whispered, "You're dead meat."

"Yes," she said, "he is very attractive." Max introduced himself politely. Green eyes. I smiled and touched him casually on his forearm, like I'd read in a magazine. Santina beamed madly and I thought her head might explode.

"Max works at Bear, Stearns," she bubbled. "He's a banker."

He turned red. He wouldn't have been embarrassed if he didn't care. Hmmm, I thought. My eyes traveled down the front of him. White Converse. A babe with a job. Could it be possible? I wondered.

"I've wanted to meet you," he said. Good voice.

"Max was just passing through when you came in. Imagine the luck."

I smiled my want-me smile and said, "Luck's got nothing to do with it."

A DEADLINE FOR MURDER

VALERIE FRANKEL

The first novel introducing Wanda
Mallory, P.I., the tough-talking,
chain-smoking, funky-chic owner
of the *Do It Right Detective Agency*
in Times Square, New York City.

From trendy Soho restaurants to
gritty Times Square bars, Wanda
and her photographer-sidekick
Alex Beaudine are tracking an
X-rated murderer who's leaving
hardcore clues.

Available from Pocket Books

POCKET
BOOKS

503